ROCKETSHIP

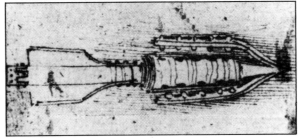

A rocket-like missile conceived by Leonardo da Vinci about 1500.

ROCKET

SHIP

An Incredible Voyage
Through Science Fiction
and Science Fact
Written By
Robert Malone
Art Editor
Jean Claude Suarès

Editor
William E. Maloney

Designer
Seymour Chwast
with Richard Mantel

HARPER & ROW, PUBLISHERS
New York, Hagerstown, San Francisco, London

A Push Pin Press Book

𝓟𝓟𝓟 A PUSH PIN PRESS BOOK
PRODUCED FOR HARPER & ROW, PUBLISHERS, INC.

Push Pin Press

Producer: Jean-Claude Suarès
Editorial Director: William E. Maloney
Design Director: Seymour Chwast

FIRST EDITION

Designed by Seymour Chwast

ISBN 0-06-012851-8
LC 77-261

About This Book

Man's impatience with his earthbound state led him to envision himself in flight. It created myths like Daedalus and Icarus and other flights of fantasy and imagination. It led, finally, to the most fantastic vision of all—escaping the earth's gravity itself, lured by curiosity to other worlds in space.

We can now float, walk, ride in space. We can look back at our planet and see it as an object for the first time. The rocketship has carried us on a voyage to new perspectives, new images, new worlds. In this book, we'll look at how we got there.

Contents

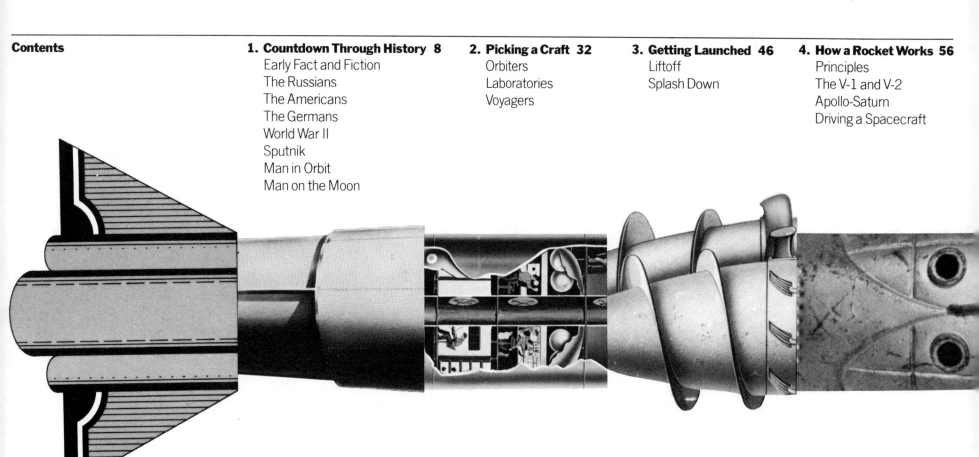

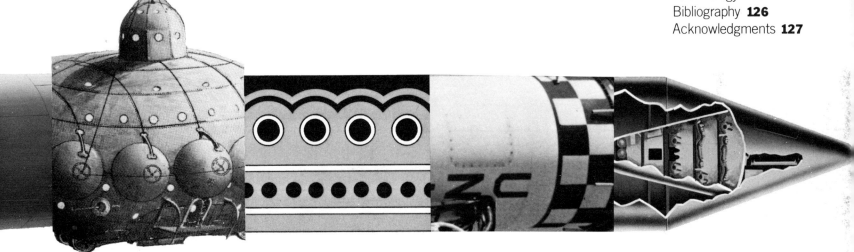

1. COUNTDOWN THROUGH HISTORY

An illustrated arsenal of 19th century weapons displays a variety of solid fuel military rockets, a rocket-launching caisson, cross sections of warheads, as well as propellant manufacturing methods and storage techniques.

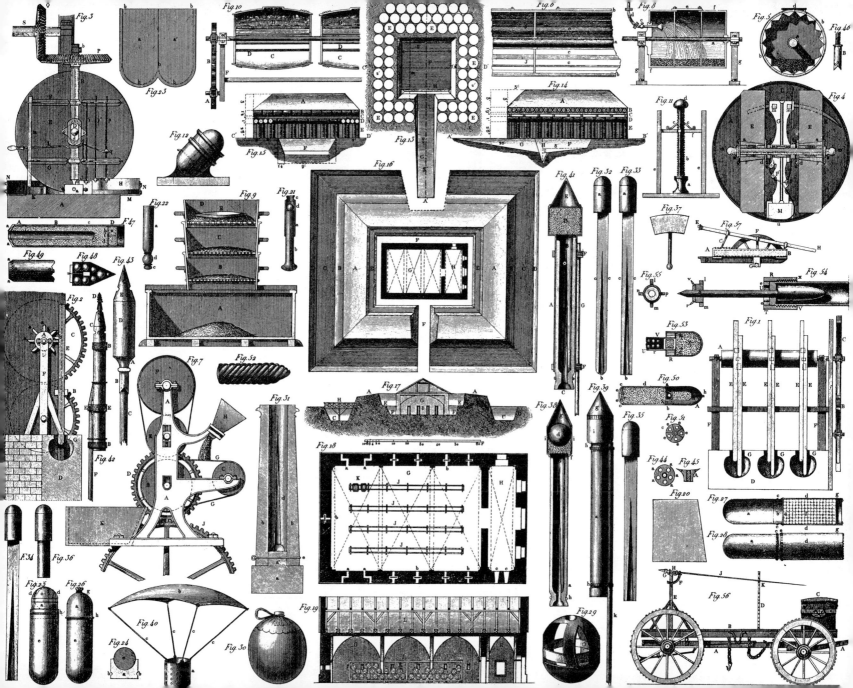

Renaissance man looks out in wonder into a universe of heavenly spheres. He sees a Biblical vision of wheels within wheels, symbolic of order in the universe.

Countdown Through History

The rocket gets its name from the Italian word "rochetta" which means lance cover. This is fitting since virtually all early rockets were used as weapons. The origins of the rocket remain shrouded in the mists of time. Twelfth century sources describe Chinese and European use of black powder devices. These were probably fueled by sulphurous mixtures containing resin and pitch (or charcoal) combined with the oxidizer saltpeter.

Paper and bamboo tubes, propelled by "slow-burning" gunpowder, may have been used as early as 1232, at the siege of K'ai-fung-fu in China. By leaving one end of a tube open, the force created by the burning powder could direct "flying fire" at the enemy. The reaction engine had thus been invented before its principle was comprehended. This principle is, of course, embodied in Newton's third law of motion: "Every action has an equal and opposite reaction."

By the mid-13th century men like Roger Bacon and Albertus Magnus wrote of "Greek fire" rockets. About 1500, Leonardo da Vinci in Italy and Wan-Hu in China turned their attention to rockets. Leonardo sketched and described a rocket that can be said to have two stages, the first stage being propelled by gun powder from a cannon. He believed the rocket could reach an altitude of three miles. In China, legend has it that Wan Hu built a rocket kite capable of carrying a man. It was powered by 47 rockets. Legend also has it that he was blown to smithereens.

By the beginning of the 17th century, speculation had already turned to space travel. Bishop Francis Godwin wrote *The Man in the Moon* in 1638. His hero, Orlando Furioso, took off for the Moon aided by a flight of captive wild geese. A contemporary of Godwin, John Wilkins wrote *Discovery of a New World*, a more factual description of space travel. Wilkins even grappled with the problem of weightlessness. The intrepid Cyrano de Bergerac, in *A Voyage to the Moon* (1649), continued this grappling with space. With his nose for novelty, he suggested using bottles of dew which would rise with the morning sun.

During this same period, royalty was entertained in Rome, London and Paris by spectacular displays of rocketry and fireworks. The famous Ruggieri family of Italy was said to have sent animals aloft by rocket, recovering them by parachute.

By 1805, an Englishman, William Congreve, had designed a formidable arsenal of rockets as weapons, that saw action in India, and at Boulogne and Copenhagen. These engagements served as warmups for the English bombardment of Fort McHenry in Baltimore during the War of 1812. Francis Scott Key was present and wrote of "the rockets' red glare," thereby giving America its national anthem. Congreve's rockets also added to Napoleon's difficulties at Waterloo.

But the writers were far ahead of the practical scientists and weapon designers. In 1827 a science fiction spaceship was launched in *Voyage to the Moon* by Joseph Atterlay. His vehicle rose with the help of an anti-gravity material called "Lunarium." Edgar Allen Poe followed in 1835 with *Hans Pfaal-A Tale.* His hero made it to the Moon by balloon, using an apparatus that condensed the atmospheric air. In 1865 Jules Verne gave the world the now-familiar *From the Earth to the Moon,* which featured a rocket-like missile carrying three astronauts shot to the Moon by a huge cannon. The fictional launch site, Tampa, Florida came prophetically close to the real Moon-launch site, Cape Canaveral, less than 150 miles away. Verne managed to give his readers a keen sense of what it might be like to travel to the Moon. On a smaller scale, the Rev. Edward Everett Hale, Chaplain to the U.S Senate, conceived of the world's first artificial satellite in 1869. It was a small moon-like object made of heat-resistant bricks to repel the Sun's destructive power.

But the more practical people were also at work. The Union Army deployed Congreve-type rockets during the Civil War.

The modern space age began toward the end of the 19th century. The Russian scientist Konstantin Tsiolkovsky worked out the theoretical principles of space flight using rockets. By 1903, he had solved, in principle, the problem of escape from the Earth's atmosphere and gravity. He also sketched the rudiments of liquid-propellant rockets. But his work was largely theoretical. It would fall to others to test out his ideas.

While Tsiolkovsky speculated, H. G. Wells was writing *The First Men on the Moon*. And in 1903 the Wright brothers built and flew the first airplane at Kitty Hawk. Seven years later, a young American, Robert H. Goddard, working at Clark College in Worcester, Mass., took out his first patents on multi-stage rockets. His very practical ideas involved solid and liquid propellants and the design of critical rocket engine parts. In 1919 he wrote *A Method of Reaching Extreme Altitudes*. Goddard went on to build and launch the first liquid-propellant rocket in 1926. It gained an altitude of only 120 feet. But it was an historic first, and can be identified as the legitimate grandfather of all subsequent space rockets. By 1935 his rockets had reached 7500 feet, using a gyroscope to stabilize flight. It is interesting to note that Goddard in his lifelong effort probably spent less money on his rockets than the production cost of one of today's small rocket motors.

During the late 1920s, enthusiasts in the U.S., Germany, England and Russia formed amateur rocket societies. They advanced the state of the art by their high level of interest. It was a time sobered by depression, yet elated by the fantasy of science fiction. The writer and editor Hugo Gernsback pumped out ideas and pulps at a prodigious rate. The public at large became enamored of Buck Rogers, Flash Gordon, and the potential of rocketships.

Responding to the work of Goddard and the German, Hermann Oberth, Germany saw a period of furious activity. Fritz von Opel flew the first rocket-propelled glider, and the startlingly predictive film *Girl in the Moon* was produced by Fritz Lang. All this was productive soil for a young Wernher von Braun and his group of rocket enthusiasts, whose work was funded by the German Army. It is unfortunate that so much of this activity was ultimately devoted to war.

Although our memory of World War II singles out Germany and its V-2 as the supreme rocket developer, the British used bombardment rockets and anti-aircraft rockets, the Japanese had the Ohka Kamikaze rocket plane, the Russians utilized the Katyusha artillery rocket, and the U.S. launched massive rocket salvos against the Japanese in amphibious landings.

Over 5000 German V-2 rockets were manufactured during the war. They achieved a thrust of 55,000 pounds, compared to the two or three hundred pounds of Robert Goddard's original. The V-2 was developed at Peenemunde under the technical direction of Wernher von Braun. After the war, he and his development team surrendered to U.S. forces. Both the U.S. and Russia scrambled to capture the brains and the technology of the German effort.

Dr. von Braun's work for the United States after the war was expected to assure the U.S. of immediate rocket superiority. And so it seemed, with firings of successively larger WAC and Redstone rockets. In 1955, President Eisenhower announced that the U.S. would launch an artificial satellite to commemorate the International Geophysical Year in 1958. Meanwhile the Russians had been very busy. They launched Sputnik I, the first Earth satellite, on October 4th, 1957. This is surely the heaviest 23 pounds the U.S. ever had to swallow, along with its pride.

The space race was on. It lasted until the U.S. reached the Moon with its manned Apollo landing. The cost to both nations was staggering. Rocketship development sped forward. The United States launched its first satellite on January 31, 1958. But each American launch was matched by a larger Soviet launch. And so it continued, through the 1961 Russian launch of Yuri Gagarin, the first man in space; then John Glenn's 1962 Mercury orbital flight; then the 1964 three-man Russian Voskhod; then the U.S. Gemini in 1965; then the Soviet and American space walks; and finally the triumphant Apollo landings on the Moon in 1969.

During this period imaginations were stimulated by the *Star Trek* television series and the mind-boggling space film *2001: A Space Odyssey*. Americans were overwhelmed by technical accomplishments, and ate breakfast to the sounds of NASA countdowns. (Interestingly, the concept of counting backward to liftoff—10, 9, 8, 7, 6, etc.—originated in a Fritz Lang science fiction movie.) The trips of Apollo to the Moon were climactic in ways we still do not comprehend.

By the 1970s people had learned a new vocabulary of space and rocket flight. The competition between the U.S. and Russia had evolved into a sharing of resources and knowledge, symbolized by the Apollo Soyuz link-up. Skylab went up, Viking flew to Mars, and we now have the prospect of shuttle service to and from space, and perhaps combined U.S. and Soviet exploration.

The planets and the stars await our future visits.

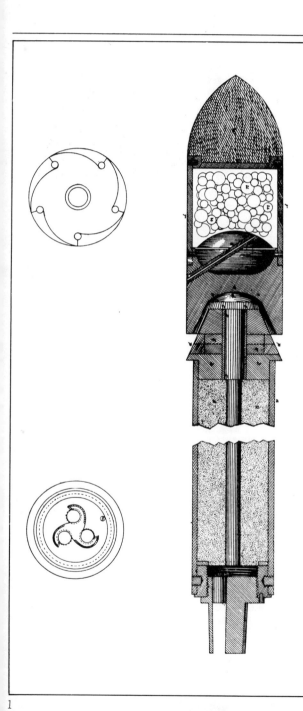

1. A section of the American "McDonald's Hale" war rocket in the style of the British designer Congreve, showing the lower solid fuel compartment and an explosive warhead. A Hale rocket was used by the United States in 1846, in the Mexican War. It was distinguished by its ability to produce a stabilizing spin, which was one step beyond the use of guide sticks and kept the rocket on course.

2. A 16th century military rocket and launch "ramp" to help guide the rocket. This is a crude forerunner of the World War II Bazooka. The base of the ramp was made from white "tinne" plate for fire prevention.

1. A rocket-launch tube designed by Congreve is stabilized by a tripod system. The British used it in India and the Orient. Oddly, the Indians had used rockets quite successfully against the British during an engagement years before, in 1792.
2. This Congreve rocket-launcher was equipped with an elevation device and had a battery of eight tubes for rapid-fire launch.

1

1. For a Moon launch, Jules Verne envisioned a 900 foot launch "cannon." He described it in his novel *From the Earth to the Moon.*
2. The cannon fired a 20,000 pound spacecraft which had a bullet-like conical nose containing three astronauts bound for the Moon. Inspection of the Verne spacecraft here gets a 4.0 rating from construction workers and crew members.
3. A still from Méliès' 1902 French film *Voyage dans la Lune.* The craft is designed in the tradition of the Verne command capsule. The explorers give obvious witness to their pride of ownership.

2

1. The Russian space pioneer Konstantin Tsiolkovsky. (1857-1935).
2. Tsiolkovsky made this sketch of a jet-propelled spacecraft. It is driven by the firing of projectiles from the cannon on the right. Four cosmonauts are depicted floating free in space. Tsiolkovsky mixed science with science fiction, and fired the imaginations of generations of Russian space enthusiasts.
3. Tsiolkovsky envisioned a space station with: 1. A closed ecological system (note trees); 2. A laboratory area; 3. Passage to living areas; 4. Living areas; 5. Docking Mechanism.

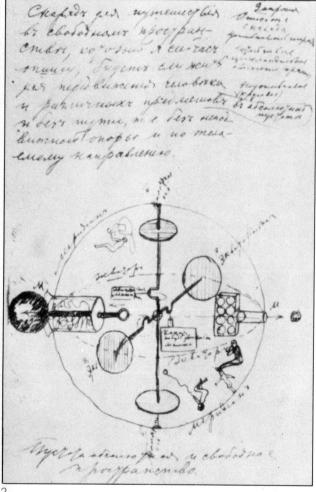

2

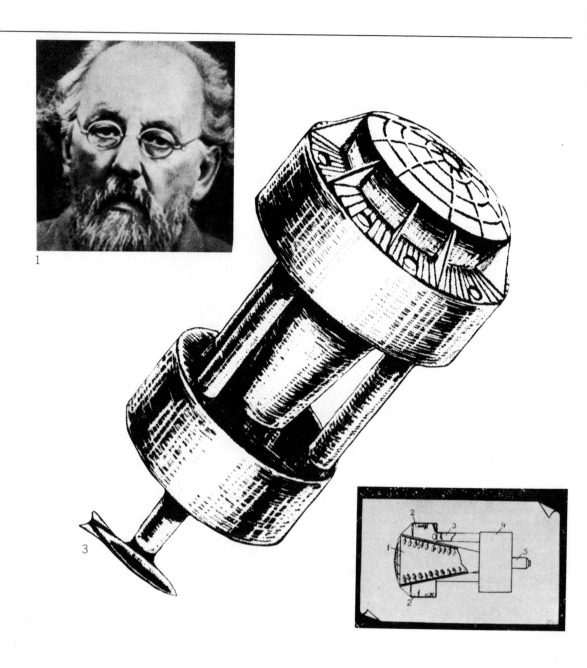

1

3

1. Edwin Pynchon's 1893 Air Ship used a "reaction engine" for propulsion. Presumably it burns a mixture of forced air (note the fans) and an unidentified fuel from the tanks above. The idea of a rocket-propelled airship is by no means a closed issue, as any reader of *Popular Science* over the past 30 years is aware.
2. Paul Maiwurm's fanciful Cyclonic Rocket depends on four rocket engines, unusual rotating tubular wings (wouldn't the whole vehicle tend to rotate?), scoop propellers and happy pilots. Obviously it's a California first.

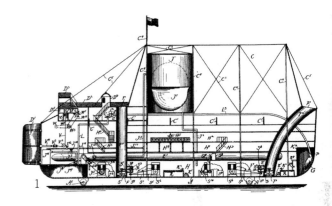

1

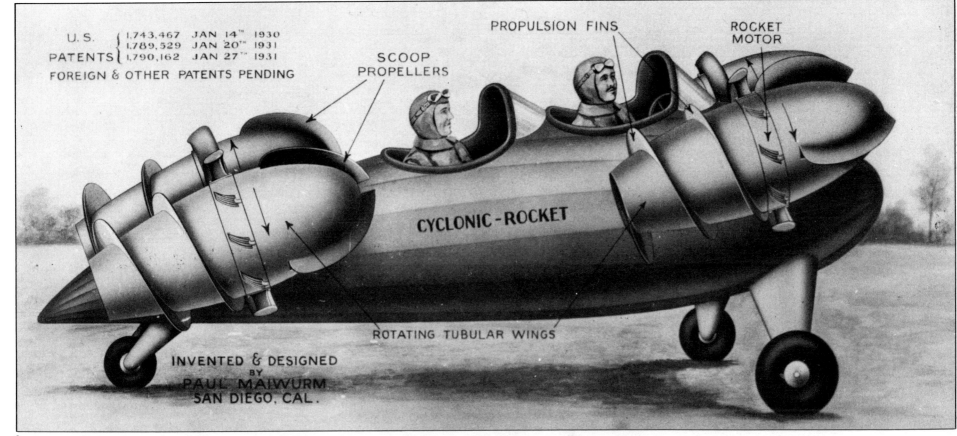

2

1

2

3

1. Robert H. Goddard (1882-1945). He is considered the father of modern rocketry.
2. Goddard poses beside a 1925 double-action rocket. By this time Goddard had solved the problem of propellant-pumping, crucial to liquid-fueled rockets. By the time of his death he held 200 patents and had established the foundation for modern rocket development.
3. Goddard launched this rocket in 1937 during his experiments in the New Mexico desert. His work was being partly financed by the Guggenheim Foundation.

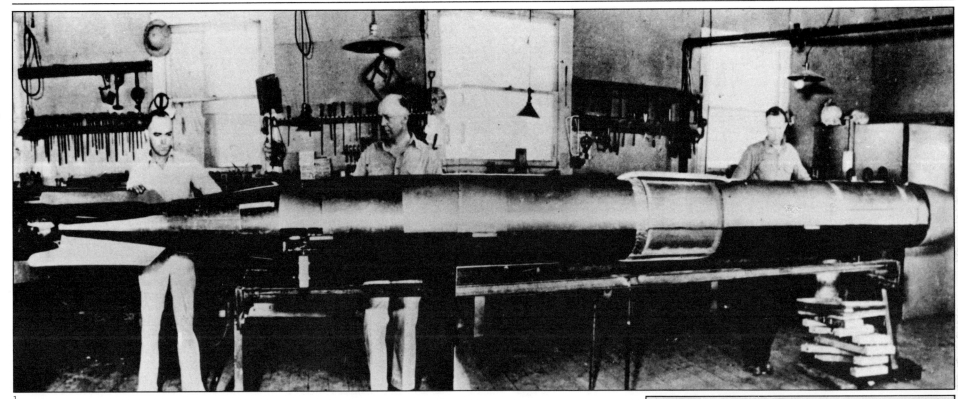

1. A composite photograph shows Goddard's 1941 rocket under construction at his Mescalero Ranch in New Mexico (the same state where five years later the first America V-2 would be launched). Two helpers and Goddard's wife, Esther, constituted his entire crew. This historic rocket can be seen at the National Air and Space Museum in Washington, D.C. Goddard later commented: "It is practically identical with the German V-2 rocket" (which was then being secretly developed in Germany).
2. A 1935 Goddard combustion chamber and nozzle shows the hydraulic steering vane assembly. The rocket's casing has been removed.

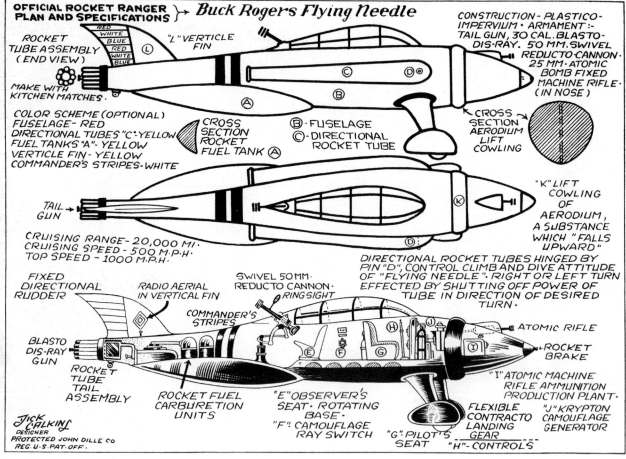

OFFICIAL ROCKET RANGER PLAN AND SPECIFICATIONS ➤ *Buck Rogers Flying Needle*

ROCKET TUBE ASSEMBLY (END VIEW)

RED WHITE BLUE RED WHITE BLUE — L

"L" VERTICLE FIN

MAKE WITH KITCHEN MATCHES.

COLOR SCHEME (OPTIONAL)
FUSELAGE - RED
DIRECTIONAL TUBES "C"- YELLOW
FUEL TANKS "A"- YELLOW
VERTICLE FIN - YELLOW
COMMANDER'S STRIPES - WHITE

CROSS SECTION ROCKET FUEL TANK (A)

(B) - FUSELAGE
(C) - DIRECTIONAL ROCKET TUBE

CONSTRUCTION - PLASTICO-IMPERVIUM · ARMAMENT :- TAIL GUN, 30 CAL. BLASTO-DIS-RAY. 50 MM. SWIVEL REDUCTO-CANNON · 25 MM · ATOMIC BOMB FIXED MACHINE RIFLE · (IN NOSE)

CROSS SECTION AERODIUM LIFT COWLING

TAIL GUN

CRUISING RANGE - 20,000 MI.
CRUISING SPEED - 500 M.P.H.
TOP SPEED - 1000 M.P.H.

"K" LIFT COWLING OF AERODIUM, A SUBSTANCE WHICH "FALLS UPWARD"

FIXED DIRECTIONAL RUDDER

RADIO AERIAL IN VERTICAL FIN

COMMANDER'S STRIPES

SWIVEL 50 MM. REDUCTO CANNON · RING SIGHT

DIRECTIONAL ROCKET TUBES HINGED BY PIN "D", CONTROL CLIMB AND DIVE ATTITUDE OF "FLYING NEEDLE". RIGHT OR LEFT TURN EFFECTED BY SHUTTING OFF POWER OF TUBE IN DIRECTION OF DESIRED TURN.

ATOMIC RIFLE

BLASTO DIS-RAY GUN

ROCKET TUBE TAIL ASSEMBLY

ROCKET FUEL CARBURETION UNITS

"E" OBSERVER'S SEAT · ROTATING BASE ·
"F" CAMOUFLAGE RAY SWITCH

"G" PILOT'S SEAT
"H" - CONTROLS

ROCKET BRAKE

"I" ATOMIC MACHINE RIFLE AMMUNITION PRODUCTION PLANT ·

FLEXIBLE CONTRACTO LANDING GEAR

"J" KRYPTON CAMOUFLAGE GENERATOR

JICK CALKINS DESIGNER
PROTECTED JOHN DILLE CO
REG. U.S. PAT. OFF.

1

1. A Buck Rogers spacecraft called the "Flying Needle" is armed to the teeth, and even sports an atomic rifle. The source for such imagery was obviously based much more on airplane designs of the 1930s than anything current in rocket development at that time.
2. The Buck Rogers film serial gave youth (and adult fans) a ready-built space world. It was complete with cabins (detailed with a nautical ship's wheel) and endless encounters for Buck and his party with evil-doers in the universe.

1. Oberth's drawing for his Modell E Rocket, demonstrating his rocket in cross-section. Oberth, author of *The Rocket into Planetary Space* and *The Road to Space Travel*, was Germany's leading rocket theoretician in the 1930s.
2. The Magdeburg rocket is prepared for launch. It was built by Rudolf Nebel and Herbert Schafer in Germany in the 1930s. On one of its 1933 launches, it flew 1000 feet horizontally. After further development it made a 3000 foot vertical flight. The group was made up of members of the pre-war VfR (Society for Space Travel), pioneers inspired by Oberth and Willy Ley.
3. An Oberth rocket being recovered by parachute. Note that the nose cone is missing. It was ejected to allow for the opening of the parachute.

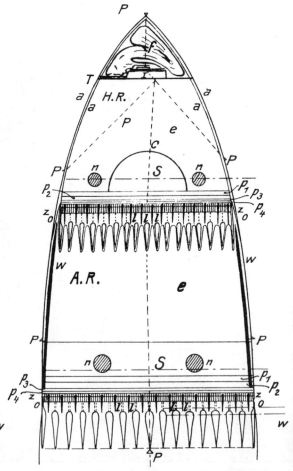

2

3

1. Launch pad, spacecraft and gantry from the 1929 film *Frau im Mond* (Girl in the Moon) by Fritz Lang. The set was based on information and advice provided by Hermann Oberth. *Frau in Mond* now appears to have been very prophetic for its time, a tribute to Oberth's predictive skill. Not until the modern films *2001: A Space Odyssey* and *Star Wars* would such technological sophistication be lavished on a space film.
2. A model of the interior of the spacecraft from *Frau im Mond*. It depicts the crew's compartment and the second stage engine and fuel shortage.
3. The *Frau im Mond* crew sprawl (incapacitated by G-forces at liftoff?) about the central ladder of the spacecraft. Set designers have attached realistic hand-holds to aid the crew in moving about the craft during weightless conditions of deep space.

1

2

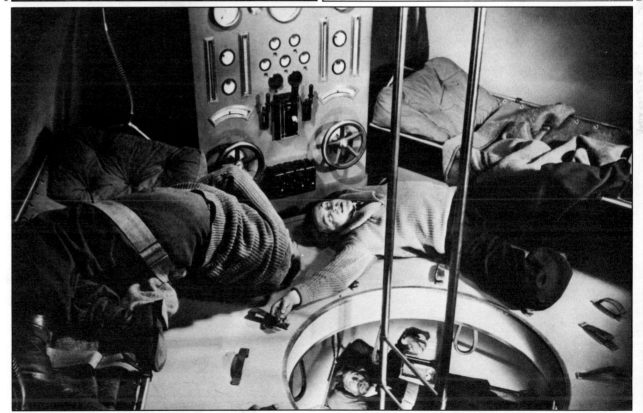

3

1. The now-famous German V-2 on a portable gantry. One of these rockets is now on display at the National Air and Space Museum. The V-2 was the brainchild of Dr. Wernher von Braun. It was developed at Peenemunde on the Baltic Sea and was first launched in October 1942. It took five minutes for this weapon to complete its 200-mile maximum journey. Von Braun's V-2 went beyond Goddard in technical development, and can be considered the first large-scale successful liquid-fueled rocket. It became the prototype for nearly all subsequent rockets.
2. The Natter Bp-20 was a 19-foot German aircraft that utilized two solid-propellant JATO (Jet Assisted Take Off) units. Ground-controlled radar brought the craft to within one mile of its target. The pilot was then to fire his 28 small rocket weapons, which can be seen in the nose section. After firing, the pilot was supposed to bail out. Natter was a flop.

1

2

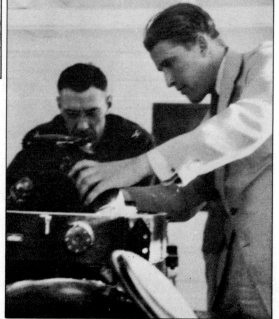

1. The first firing of an American V-2 took place at White Sands
   Proving Grounds, New Mexico, on April 16, 1946. It was a prototype of our next 20 years of rocket development. In this photo
   the V-2 is being raised on its gantry for a static check out. The
   next step in the V-2's development was an added stage called
   the Wac Corporal. It was referred to as the Bumper series. The
   V-2's warhead had been replaced by scientific measuring
   instruments.
2. Wernher von Braun surrendered to United States forces in May
   1945. By September he was in America, hard at work at Fort
   Bliss, Texas. He worked on modified V-2's which had been cap-
   tured by American forces. His contribution to the development
   of rocketry and space travel (aided by a devoted team of associ-
   ates) can only be compared to that of Goddard and possibly
   Tsiolkovsky.

1

2

1. Sputnik galvanized the world on October 4, 1957, as the Russians announced the first orbiting artificial satellite. It weighed 84 pounds and carried an instrument package for analyzing the Earth's upper atmosphere. Five months later (for NASA it felt more like five years), the United States launched a small, 18 pound satellite, Explorer I. It did, however, have excellent miniaturized instruments.
2. The American launch, of Explorer, was followed on March 17, 1958 by the successful orbital launch of the Vanguard satellite, here being lifted by the three-stage Vanguard rocket developed by the Martin Company.
3. The Vanguard helped put America back into the space race with the Russians, and yielded information on the Earth's magnetic field and radiation belt.

3

1. The Russian Yuri Gagarin (1934-1968) had the unique distinction of being the first man to travel in space. He orbited the Earth in Vostok 1 on April 12th, 1961. He died on a training flight of a MiG-15. His mission marked a giant step in space flight. The American response came from President Kennedy, who announced that the United States would put a man on the moon within the decade.
2. Astronaut John Glenn in the cabin of the Mercury spacecraft during simulation testing. Mercury was the first manned spacecraft that the United States put into orbital flight. Glenn orbited the Earth three times on February 20, 1962.
3. Glenn was an instant hero. His ticker tape parade up Broadway in New York City outdid in scale even that given Charles Lindbergh.

1. A scene from the 1953 science fiction movie *Spaceways* shows an interesting concept for a three-stage space rocket. Imagination continued to leap ahead of reality in space travel.
2. *2001: A Space Odyssey.* This masterpiece of science fiction (filmed in 1968) combined the talents of filmmaker Stanley Kubrick and author Arthur C. Clarke. They created a most plausible set of images for future space travel. As early as 1945 Clarke has suggested the development of artificial satellites for use in a world communications system. In this scene from *2001*, the two Jupiter-bound astronauts aboard the "Discovery" meet for a conference in an EVA module, hopefully beyond the hearing range of the on-board computer HAL, which wants to take over complete control of the ship.

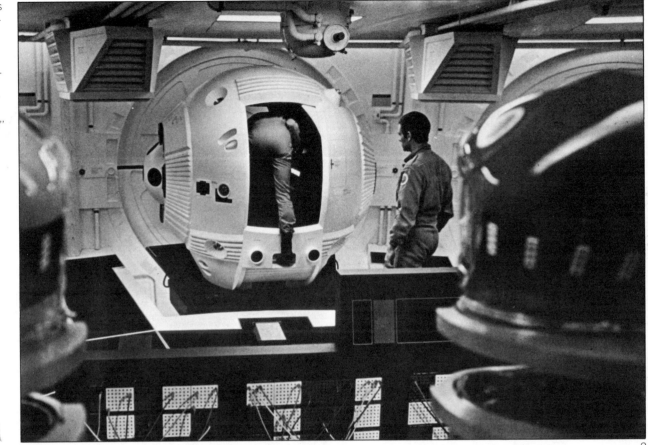

1

2

1. Front page of The New York Times reporting the first manned Moon landing on July 16, 1969. The dream became a reality as the Lunar Module touched down, allowing Neil Armstrong to walk on the Moon.
2. Astronaut Harrison Schmitt of the Apollo 17 mission collects samples of rock and rock chips during a walk at the Taurus-Littrow landing site. His camera and back-pack, though bulky, don't seem to impede his progress.

1

2

Fact Follows Fantasy

Science fiction writers had early on envisioned rockets as mail carriers. Experiments were conducted in Austria in 1928 and in Germany in the 1930s. In 1934 a rocket was loaded with mail on the Outer Hebrides island of Scarp. The rocket was aimed for the neighboring island of Harris. It exploded on the launch pad and the mail was badly singed. Mail did make it to the Moon, however.

2. PICKING A CRAFT

A sampling of ships from the fleet of Buck Rogers includes the Martian-Venutian Tri-Blast Special. These wondrous configurations pre-date in form the Enterprise of *Star Trek* and *2001*'s Discovery. The art is highly prized by collectors.

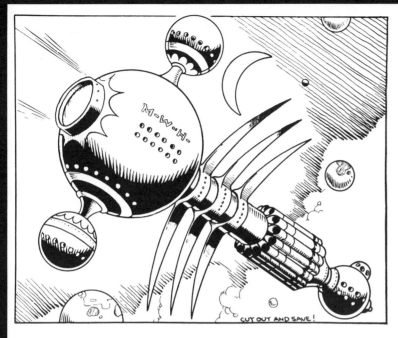

CUT OUT AND SAVE!

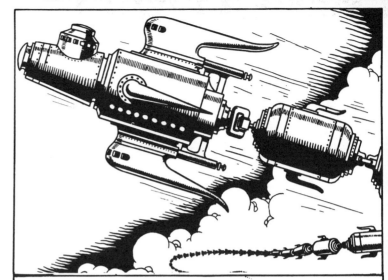

INTERPLANETARY FREIGHT TRAIN, PONDEROUSLY WINDING ITS SLUGGISH WAY THROUGH THE OUTER-SPACES AT 300 MILES PER MINUTE —— CAPABLE OF DRAWING 6500 "CARS"! CUT OUT AND SAVE!

THE "SUPER-TWIN INTERPLANETARY COMET"— 44,500 H.P. - GYRO-STABILIZED-ACCOMODATING 1200 PASSENGERS AND A CREW OF **200** MEN. CRUISING SPEED 3000 MILES PER HOUR.

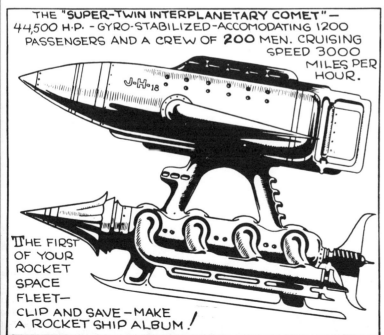

THE FIRST OF YOUR ROCKET SPACE FLEET— CLIP AND SAVE—MAKE A ROCKET SHIP ALBUM!

" MARTIAN – VENUTIAN TRI-BLAST SPECIAL NO.DT12—MC 11 " !
SPEED — 800 MILES PER SECOND
TYPE — MAIL SHIP
HORSEPOWER 4,500,601
CREW-10 OFFICERS
100 ABLE SPACEMEN

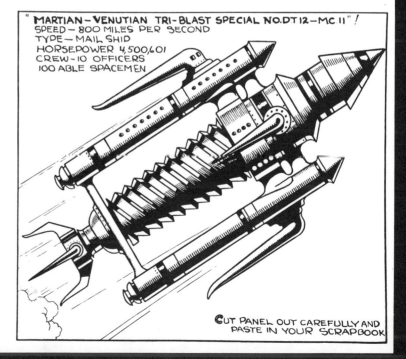

CUT PANEL OUT CAREFULLY AND PASTE IN YOUR SCRAPBOOK

Picking a Craft

The requirements of the mission dictate the design and selection of the craft.

The United States and the Soviet Union have created spacecraft for a wide variety of missions. You'll find them illustrated in this book.

But first, it's a good idea to define the common terms used. For practical, working purposes NASA uses two separate terms to describe the giant machine you see sitting on the launching pad at the Kennedy Space Center. They talk about the "spacecraft" and the "vehicle."

The spacecraft carries the payload in space, be it instruments or astronauts. Examples are the Earth-orbiting Mercury and Gemini, as well as the Apollo.

The vehicle, in NASA parlance, is the big rocket which boosts the spacecraft off the pad and gives it enough speed to achieve orbit, or to escape the Earth's gravity. These rockets are also called "boosters." Examples are the Atlas, which lifted the Mercury, and the Titan, which lifted the Gemini spacecraft into orbit, and the huge Saturn which lifted Apollo on its moon flight. Sections of these big rockets are often "staged," that is, stacked one atop the other. When the first stage has lifted the craft to a certain height and expended its fuel, it is jettisoned and the next stage ignites. Once these stages have done their job, they usually fall back into the Earth's atmosphere. The spacecraft is then on its own, maneuvering with its small, on-board rockets which can be fired in short bursts to change speed and direction.

1

1. The X-15 research airplane had a rocket engine. It was a suborbital craft that allowed for much-needed testing of men and materials in rocket-powered flight.
2. A Mercury spacecraft sits atop its Redstone booster. It was equipped with a 16-foot escape tower system which could lift the craft free from its huge booster rockets if there was an explosion or malfunction at liftoff.

2

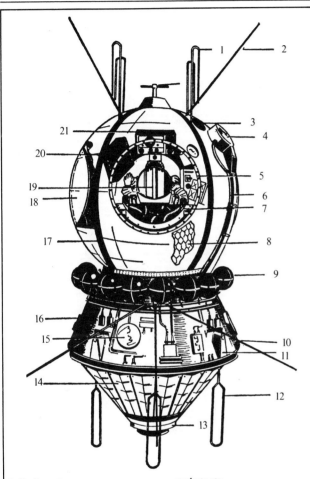

1. The Vostok spacecraft in diagram form. This craft carried Gagarin during his first orbit of the earth in 1961.
2. Unlike the Mercury spacecraft, the Gemini did not need an escape tower since it had ejection seats built into the craft. (A risky exit, to say the least.) The Gemini contained two astronauts in slightly more comfort than Mercury's single astronaut enjoyed.

1. Radio antennae.
2. Communications antennae.
3. Capsule porthole.
4. Multi-adaptor plug for connections between capsule and instrument section.
5. Opening for hatch-cover. Explosive bolts jettison hatch cover during parachute descent of capsule, so that ejector seat can come out.
6. Recessed cable.
7. Ejector seat with parachute and cosmonaut.
8. Honeycomb heat shield (exposed).
9. Gas containers for steering rockets etc.
10. Antenna for communication with earth.
11. Antenna for orbit measurements.
12. Antenna (telemetry).
13. Retro-rocket.
14. Shutters for temperature control.
15. Hatch to instrument section.
16. Instrument section.
17. Steel bands connecting capsule to instrument section.
18. Parachute hatch.
19. Cosmonaut's helmet.
20. Switch panel.
21. Instrument panel.

1

2

1. The American Space Shuttle (about the size of a DC-9 jetliner) is the reusable spacecraft that will become a workhorse in flights between Earth and orbital space stations. Its storage area is large enough to hold a Greyhound bus or, hopefully, a more sensible payload. It will jettison its solid fuel rocket boosters at about a 25-mile altitude, for water recovery. After its mission is completed in space, the Shuttle will return to Earth, where it will land like an airplane.

2. This strange looking craft is called a "lifting body." It is a hybrid: half airplane, half spacecraft. It was developed by Martin Marietta to explore the launching and re-entry problems that would be encountered by the Space Shuttle (then in its planning stages). It flew several times (after being dropped from a mother plane) and proved aerodynamically stable enough to land under complete pilot control.

3. Hugo Gernsback's 1930s science fiction spacecraft. Note the Earth in the far left corner. Could it be that Gernsback, in his imaginary world of science fiction, had invented the flying saucer?

2

3

1. How the Americans and the Russians met in space: A diagram of the Apollo-Soyuz, demonstrating the position of the various modules that make up the cluster system that permitted American and Russian crews to visit from one craft to the other. The docking module has two airlocks. The atmospheres of the Apollo and the Soyuz modules were not similar (either as to chemical mixture or pressure per square inch) but this was no great problem. The Americans will adopt the Russian atmosphere in the future.
2. An illustration by Paul Fyeld depicting the historic Apollo-Soyuz rendezvous in space. Locked together, the two craft extended to a length of 70 feet.
3. The Skylab space station cluster as it was photographed in 1973 from Skylab 4 command and service modules. Note the solar shield which was hand-deployed by a crew to replace a shield damaged in the launch. A solar panel on the left side failed to deploy. Despite these mishaps, scientific and human engineering experiments were an outstanding success. The third crew manning Skylab worked in the craft for 84 days, travelling over 34,000,000 miles.

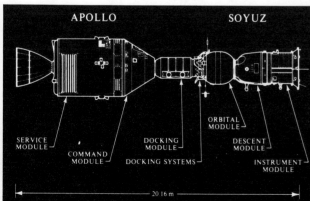

APOLLO   SOYUZ

SERVICE MODULE

COMMAND MODULE

DOCKING MODULE

DOCKING SYSTEMS

ORBITAL MODULE

DESCENT MODULE

INSTRUMENT MODULE

20.16 m

1

2

1. Simulation testing of a Viking spacecraft. Viking traveled 460 million miles to Mars and landed safely, after deploying parachutes which braked its landing in the thin Martian atmosphere. The pictures it sent back of the Red Planet were incredible in their detail. Its analysis of the Martian environment has failed to reveal any form of life as we know it.
2. An artist's conception of an orbiting telescope with a 120-inch aperture lens. The advantage of having a telescope in space is that the view through its lens is undistorted by the Earth's atmosphere.
3. This space tug is envisioned for operation in Earth orbit. It would provide a continuously available work-station at an orbital level, making it unnecessary to launch individual craft whenever the need arises. Its arms resemble those of the space pods in *2001*.

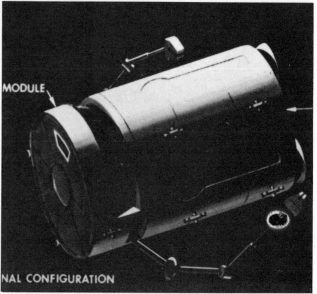

1. Craft that venture into deep space, like the fictional Enterprise of *Star Trek*, will have to be a combination of lab/workshop and ship/hotel. Too heavy to be lifted into space, they would be assembled in parts at an orbital level. Shuttle and tugs would bring materials from Earth (or even the Moon) for construction. The "Astronef 732," conceived by artist/designer François Dallegret has as its seventh stage a chapel. Its destination is Mars, carrying 7,000 passengers distributed in a space craft the height of the Empire State building. Dallegret conservatively estimates the cost at a modest seven billion dollars. Surely it would cost one hundred times that, since a 1966 NASA estimate placed the cost of the Apollo program at over 23 billion dollars, Gemini at well over a billion, and Mercury at about 400 million.

2. A model of the Apollo spacecraft allows for a closeup view of the service module, with its reaction control system. Clusters of small rockets are able to fire in short bursts in any of four directions (note simulated firings) for in-flight course changes and altitude control.

3. The Apollo diagram displays the service, command and scientific instrument modules.

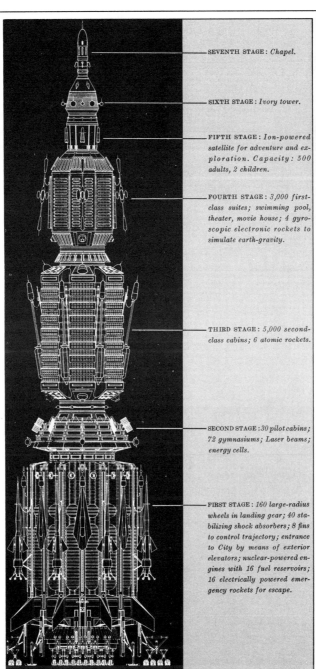

SEVENTH STAGE : *Chapel.*

SIXTH STAGE : *Ivory tower.*

FIFTH STAGE : *Ion-powered satellite for adventure and exploration. Capacity: 500 adults, 2 children.*

FOURTH STAGE : *3,000 first-class suites; swimming pool, theater, movie house; 4 gyroscopic electronic rockets to simulate earth-gravity.*

THIRD STAGE : *5,000 second-class cabins; 6 atomic rockets.*

SECOND STAGE : *30 pilot cabins; 72 gymnasiums; Laser beams; energy cells.*

FIRST STAGE : *160 large-radius wheels in landing gear; 40 stabilizing shock absorbers; 8 fins to control trajectory; entrance to City by means of exterior elevators; nuclear-powered engines with 16 fuel reservoirs; 16 electrically powered emergency rockets for escape.*

1

2

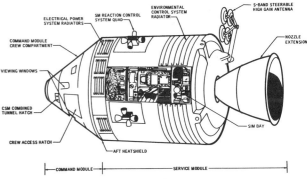

3

1. The prototype of the deep space voyager is Noah's Ark. This mid-19th century illustration by Gustave Doré depicts the Ark bathed in the light of optimism. It survived the Flood to start the world again (very economically) with just two of each species of animal. In modern times, the ark concept has once again grasped the imagination as a means to escape a world holocaust. The ark appears frequently in science fiction, where it is linked ultimately to the founding of a space colony.
2. Time marches on, and here in 1939 we have the *Startling Stories* Ark of Space. Survival still requires only two of each species. The dirigible-like voyager has the sure touch of artist Howard Brown. Portholes were very popular in the 1930s. Each animal could have a window seat. The rocket is presumably launched horizontally.
3. By 1961, the space ark is illustrated in *Fantastic Stories* as a von Braun/NASA rocket. The economy of using only two animals of each species is still preserved. The horizon beyond the launch complex looks ominous. More than a light rain is expected as we can tell by the title of the cover story, *Deluge II*.

A NOVEL OF THE FUTURE COMPLETE IN THIS ISSUE!

STARTLING STORIES

NOV.

ARK OF SPACE

15¢

A THRILLING PUBLICATION

THE FORTRESS OF UTOPIA
By JACK WILLIAMSON

A MARTIAN ODYSSEY By STANLEY G. WEINBAUM

FANTASTIC

OCTOBER   STORIES OF IMAGINATION

35¢

DELUGE II
By Robert F. Young

THE MOTHER
By David H. Keller, M.D.

LAST DRUID
By Joseph E. Kelleam

ALEX SCHOMBURG

2

3

1. *2001: A Space Odyssey*, by Stanley Kubrick and Arthur Clarke, featured a fantastic Jupiter flight voyager. It made use of the very latest in space technology, at least by 1968 movie standards. The film maintains the myth of salvation, in a regenerated life for the astronaut. But the final fate of Earth is mysteriously left hanging in the balance.

2. A voyager is under construction in the 1951 film *When Worlds Collide*. Scientists are building this ship in order to survive the expected collision between Earth and another planet. The streamlined design, in a late art deco treatment, has overtones of Flash Gordon.

3. In his 1976 novel *Rendezvous with Rama*, Arthur Clarke envisioned a gigantic cylindrical space colony which wanders into our solar system. On penetrating the vehicle, Earth investigators discover a complete ecosystem, with an atmosphere and a central sea. Though we never meet the alien voyagers (they are in a suspended state), Clarke clearly suggests that the ark concept is as popular with aliens as with ourselves. The idea of a cylindrical-shaped space station is realized in this illustration of a concept by Dr. Gerard O'Neill of Princeton. Equipped to house over 100,000 inhabitants, it used solar power for energy and lunar or asteroid materials for station construction. The teacup-shaped containers ringing the cylinder are agricultural stations. The rectangular mirrors would direct sunlight into the interior. (See page 121.)

1

2

3. GETTING LAUNCHED

The spacecraft from the
1951 movie *When Worlds
Collide*, at the moment of
launch from its great
curving ramp. This film
established a very high
standard in set design
and special effects
model-making for sci-
ence fiction films about
space.

Getting Launched

Despite technological advances in launching, the principle for getting a rocket off the ground has not changed for centuries. Before the concept of the gantry (from the Latin word for trellis), such diverse persons as da Vinci and Jules Verne had thought of using a cannon for launching. Explosion of the gunpowder in the cannon would provide first-stage power, while the barrel would provide control and direction.

Historically, both in fact and fiction, some form of guide-way has been suggested or tried. The objective is to give the rocket a firm initial direction. Early launches of military rockets were usually horizontal or slightly angled up. The idea was to gain ground distance rather than altitude. To accomplish this, use was made of rails, ramps, and tubes. (The World War II Bazooka rocket was launched from a tube.)

What distinguishes the space launch of today is the vertical position of the rocket and gantry. All the essentials of today's gantry were present, at least in principle, in Robert Goddard's 1945 New Mexico tests. Whatever evolution has occurred has been concentrated into the sub-systems, fueling apparatus, elevators for launch and vehicle crews, monitoring and check-out systems, control linkage and position, and the many safety by-products.

Rockets are usually moved onto special pads for launch. This was true of the 19th century German camera rocket. It was also true of the V-2. (For reasons of defense, they were often launched from railroad cars.) It is of course true today of the Saturn-Apollo, which is moved from the VAB (Vehicle Assembly Building) to the launch gantry by a huge caterpillar tread tractor.

Rocketships are launched through an incredibly complex series of steps. The countdown really begins with assembly and testing. One tiny mistake in assembly—an inverted valve, for example—can abort the lift-off and threaten the mission.

1

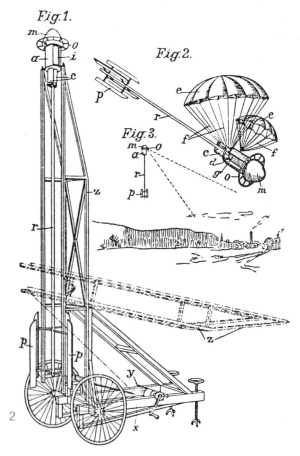

2

1. Alfred Maul's military observation camera rocket, developed for the German Army in 1906. The launcher was horse-pulled to the site closest to the area to be photographed, then the gantry was raised and the rocket launched.
2. The camera was automatically triggered, and then the rocket and camera were returned to the ground by parachute. This was a lot of effort for only one picture per launch. As airplanes came to be used for observation, development of Maul's rocket ceased. Forty years later, interest in the idea was heightened by its potential use in high altitude scientific rockets.

1. Robert Goddard (at Clark University in Massachussetts in 1915), displays a rocket chamber mounting on a simple gantry. Little attention was paid to his work at the time. By 1940 Goddard's rocket and gantry ideas began to approach our contemporary concepts.
2. The scale difference between Goddard's rocket, which was about 18 feet long, and the 1961 three-stage Saturn C-1 can be visually identified by comparing the two figures on both gantries. This truncated version of Saturn is 160 feet long, compared with its ultimate length of 363 feet. The debt of modern rocketry to Robert Goddard could not be better demonstrated.

1

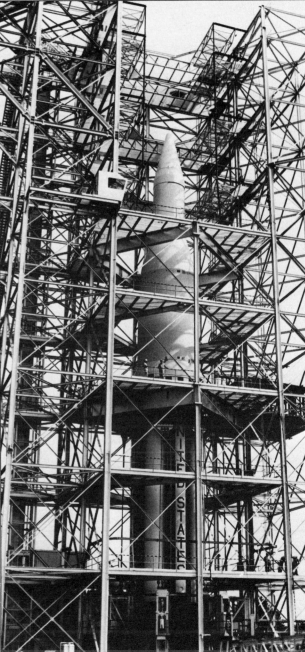

2

1. A diagram of the 1973 Skylab vehicle mobile launcher gives dramatic evidence of the size and complexity of existing launch systems. Men are too small to delineate in this drawing. The top level of the gantry rises to 380 feet, more than a third of the height of the Empire State Building.
2. At Kennedy Space Center a Saturn launch vehicle is rolled out, on its way to the launch pad for the liftoff, on July 15, 1975, of an Apollo spacecraft. The Apollo later completed a rendezvous and docking with the Russian Soyuz.

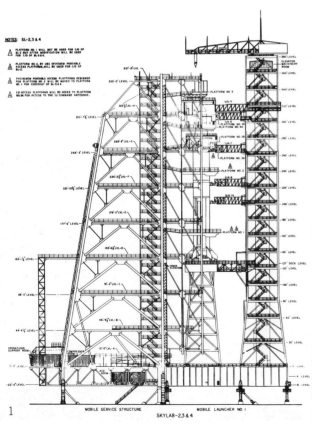

1. The work horse of Russian space flight, the 120-foot RNV (Rakyeta Nosityel Vostok) vehicle which launched the one-man Vostok spacecraft. Its cantilevered gantry is radically different from the NASA version.

Fact Follows Fantasy
When illustrator Frank Paul created the drawing for Tucker's "The Cubic City" in *Science Wonder* in 1929, he visualized a four square mile building looming larger than the World Trade Center in New York City. His building has a mere 800 floors. On a smaller scale the Vehicle Assembly Building at the Kennedy Space Center, Cape Canaveral, appears to be the son of Cubic City. It is the largest scientific building in the world, according to the *Guinness Book of Records*. Its doors must allow for the emergence of a 363 foot high Saturn V. The building measures 716 feet long, by 518 feet wide, by 460 feet high, and in itself is no mean feat of construction.

1

Getting Launched

1. The Titan 3C shoots skyward with a 20,000 pound payload of satellites to be placed in Earth orbit. The core vehicle is a Titan 2 liquid-fueled rocket. Strapped to its side are two solid propellent boosters. An automated spacecraft called Transtage is carried atop the booster. On one flight it placed eight satellites in various orbits, including a synchronous orbit 22,000 miles in space.

2. A view from about 400 feet up, looking down on the Saturn V rocket poised for the first Apollo manned flight in December, 1968. Seven previous flights, all unmanned, had proved the performance of the giant booster.

1

2

1. Alfred Maul's 1907 rocket device for releasing a parachute at the terminus of a flight. The recovery technique has become much more sophisticated, but the principle hasn't changed.
2. The creators of the Buck Rogers comic strip understood the problems of re-entry. A parachute device gets a female space-traveler out of a tight spot. Russian and American capsule recoveries will depend upon parachutes until the Space Shuttle makes returning to Earth a more "routine" affair.

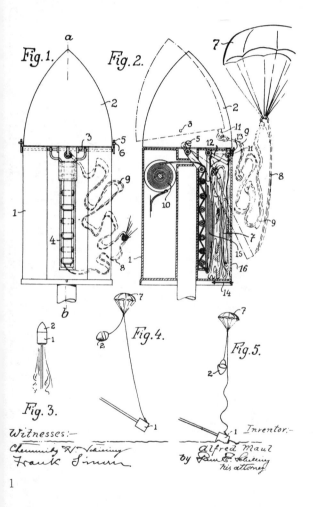

Fact Follows Fantasy

Jules Verne surely had the gift of prophesy back in 1865 when, in his novel about a Moon flight, he conjured up this splashdown and recovery. About one hundred years later, American astronauts from Apollo 14 splashed down and re-enacted the scene.

4. HOW A ROCKET WORKS

An airship with a battery-reaction engine heads for the stratosphere in this 19th century print. The inset shows explosive pellets being dropped into a triggering device. The engine is controlled from the gondola by cables.

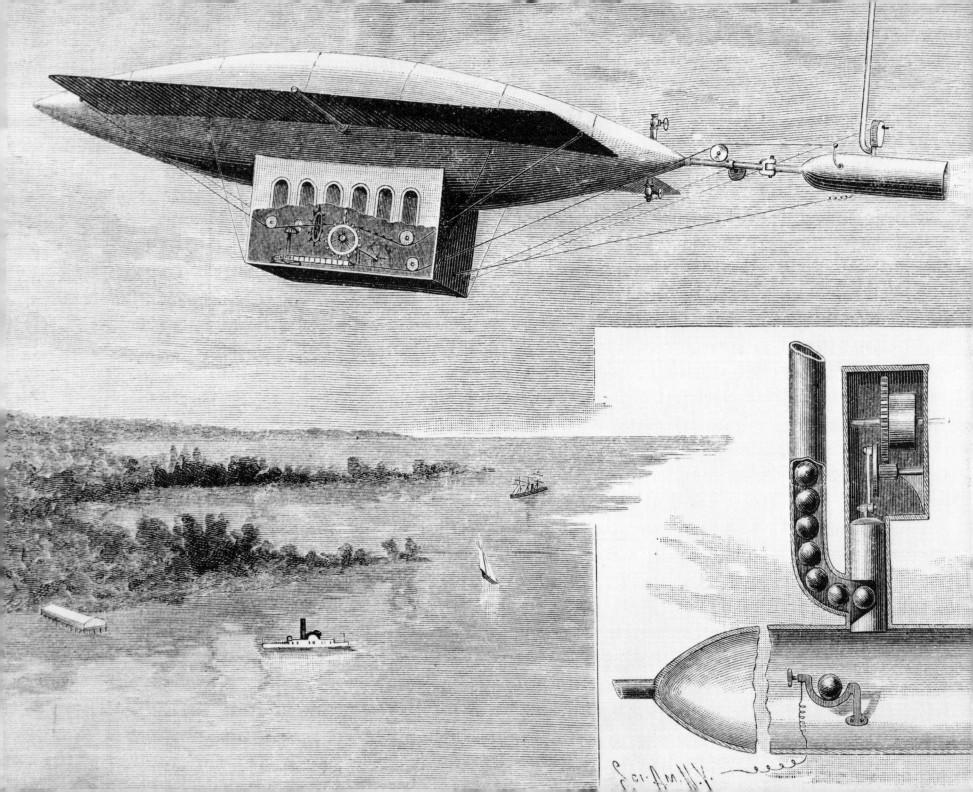

How a Rocket Works

All rockets are reaction engines, which burn either solid or liquid propellants. As we have known since Newton, if there is an action, (explosive force in this case), there is a reaction of equal magnitude in the opposite direction. This principle allows the rocket engine to create thrust.

The biggest rockets today burn two liquids: a fuel consisting of either liquid hydrogen, alchohol, or kerosine stored in one tank, and an oxidizer, such as liquid oxygen, stored in another tank. These are balance-fed by command from either a ground station or on-board computer, through a set of valves and a turbine pump system. These measure out the mix to a combustion chamber, and simultaneously cool the exhaust nozzle.

The big engines create millions of pounds of thrust. They also burn incredible amounts of fuel, almost 17 tons per second, in the case of Saturn V, America's most powerful rocket.

What's the principle difference between a rocket and a jet engine? A rocket engine can operate in the vacuum of space because oxygen is a component of the fuel mixture (the liquid oxygen mentioned above).

Once in space, and having left its staging rockets behind, a spacecraft is maneuvered by small on-board rockets which can be fired in short bursts, and then shut down until needed again. The most powerful of these on-board rockets is the retro rocket, used to slow down the craft enough to re-enter the atmosphere without burning up from heat created by friction.

1. Diagram illustrates reaction principle.
2. The World War II German V-1 is often thought of as a rocket weapon. It was not. It was a 27-foot pulse-jet vehicle, with an air intake duct to provide oxygen for combustion in the propulsion unit (rear top). The main section below contains the gyro control for steering, a warhead for killing, fuel, compressed air tanks, and battery and hydraulic control systems to control the course of its atmospheric flight. The V-1s were launched from rails and proved effective as terror weapons over London. The V-1 weighed 4,858 pounds and developed 1100 pounds of thrust, but its relatively slow speed (350 mph) made it vulnerable to fighter plane attack. The V-2 that followed was a true rocket, burning fuel and liquid oxygen. Over 1000 fell on the London area.

How the Rocket Works

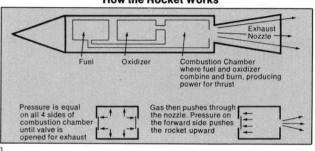

1

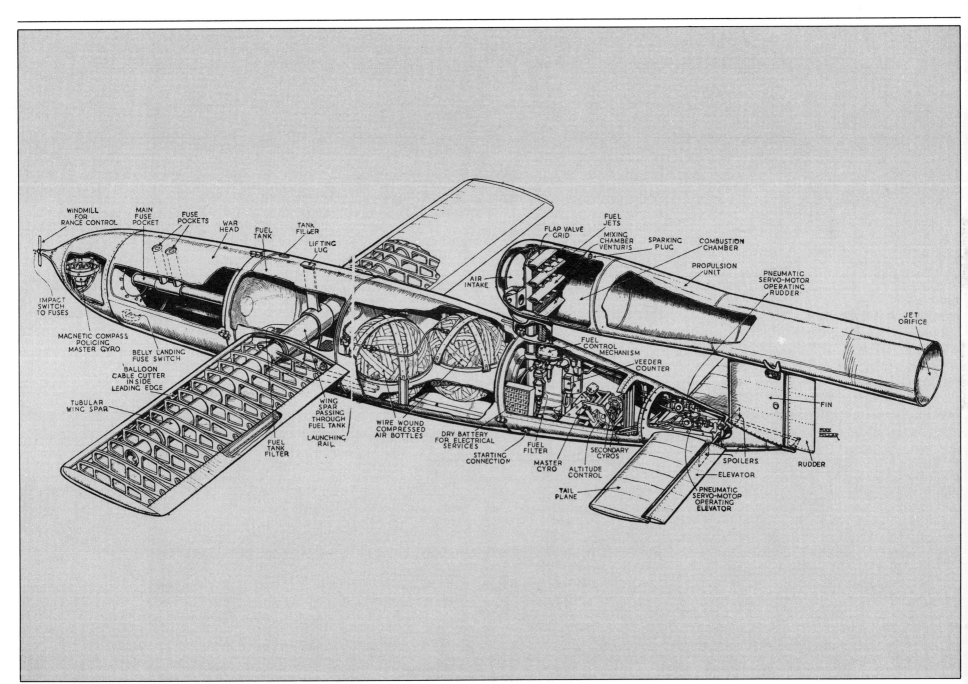

1. Saturn V is a three stage rocket. Each stage has its own fuel and engine. The first stage burns liquid oxygen and kerosene, the others liquid oxygen and liquid hydrogen. As each stage burns out, it is jettisoned, leaving finally the Apollo spacecraft with its own command, service and lunar modules which have their own on-board rocket engines. The three stages have a total of 11 engines, which lift Saturn V's more than 6 million pound weight with a combined thrust of over 9,000,000 pounds: 7,680,000 pounds of thrust in the first stage, 1,150,000 in the second and 230,000 in the third.

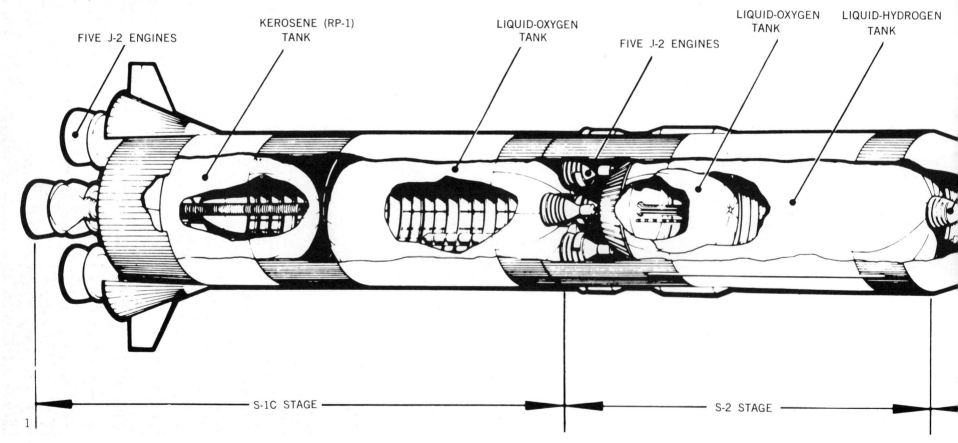

FIVE J-2 ENGINES   KEROSENE (RP-1) TANK   LIQUID-OXYGEN TANK   FIVE J-2 ENGINES   LIQUID-OXYGEN TANK   LIQUID-HYDROGEN TANK

S-1C STAGE — S-2 STAGE

1. Technicians work on the engines of the Titan booster used in the Gemini flights. Valves and piping must work under enormous heat and pressure. Failure of a component could cause a disastrous explosion of the volatile fuel and liquid oxygen.
2. The engines of the spacecraft in the movie *2001: A Space Odyssey* dwarfed in scale even the huge engines of Saturn V. Assembled in space, the Discovery is bound for Jupiter, powered by atomic fusion engines. The crew compartment was separated from the engine unit by a large distance to protect the crew from radiation generated as a byproduct of the fusion process.

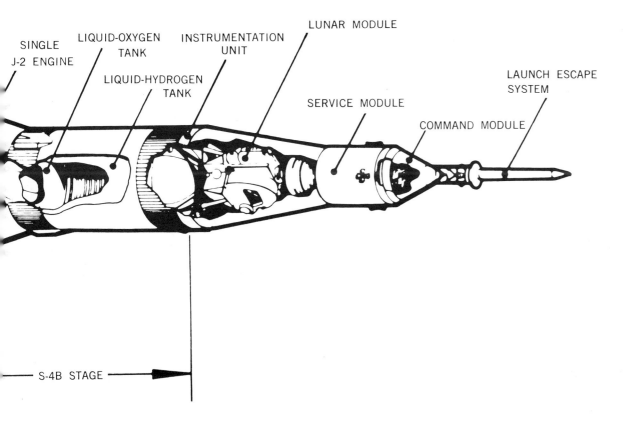

SINGLE
J-2 ENGINE

LIQUID-OXYGEN
TANK

LIQUID-HYDROGEN
TANK

INSTRUMENTATION
UNIT

LUNAR MODULE

SERVICE MODULE

COMMAND MODULE

LAUNCH ESCAPE
SYSTEM

S-4B STAGE

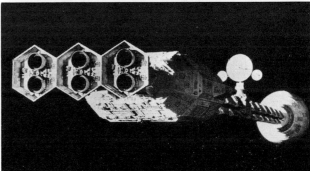

1. The control console from Paul's illustration for a *Wonder Stories Quarterly* story shows the interior space to be layed out with uncommon generosity. Naturally there's a telescreen and lots of levers and buttons to push.

2. By contrast, note the tight cockpit dimensions (like a Lotus sports car) of L. Gordon Cooper's Mercury capsule. He drives his craft using a periscope, in the Lindbergh tradition, rather than a window. He does have manual controls for course changes, using as a reference the diagrammatic globe in front of him and his panels of instruments. These give him his speed, the number of orbit, altitude, craft orientation (in reference to the earth), time, battery conditions and fuel supply. They also monitor his life-support system. This information is given to him in the form of digital read-outs, dials and warning lights.

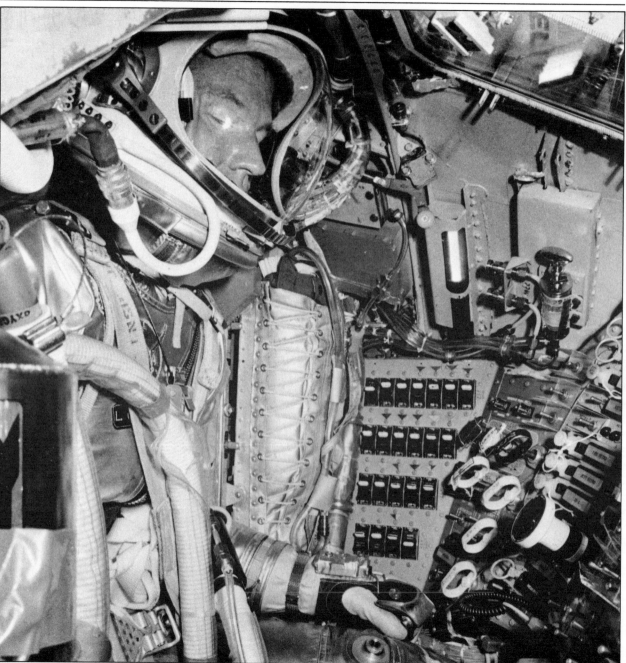

1

1. In the one-man Mercury spacecraft, all the instrumentation is located around the astronaut for his monitoring or control. He ran the whole show, working with ground control. By the time the Apollo was developed, the three astronauts divided up the chores and the responsibility, one handling capsule control, the second guidance and navigation, and the third spacecraft systems monitoring, with the instrumentation divided up between the three couches. As the spacecraft matured in design, the degree of sophistication and scale of on-board computer use increased greatly, as did the amount of available energy on board due to more efficient hydrogen fuel cells. This increase in available energy made possible far greater flexibility and range in maneuvering, and added a much greater margin of safety to the flight.

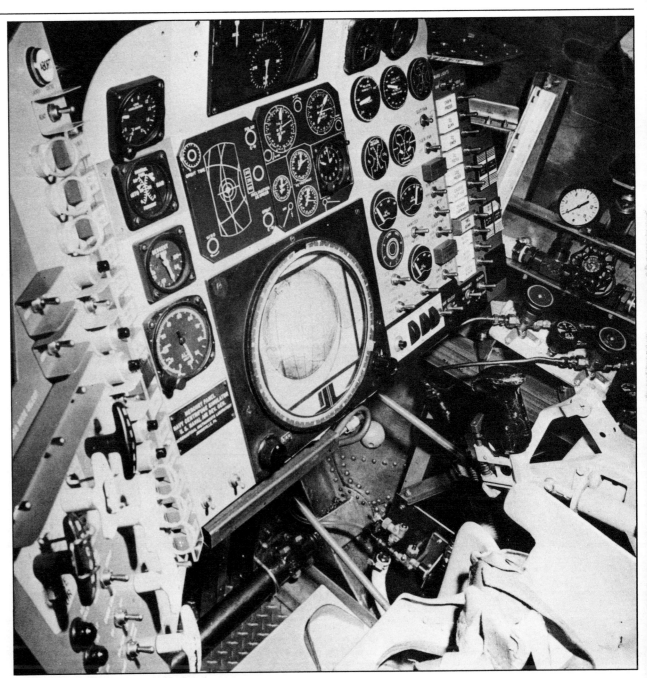

1. Each one of the Mercury, Gemini and Apollo spacecraft had its own level of flight and instrument sophistication. Astronauts Schirra and Young practice procedures.
2. Gemini utilizes two control sticks which allows for capsule steering and orientation. The first stick controls pitch, yaw and nose rotation, as well as up/down and right/left motion. The second stick controls the direction (up, down, sideways) of the entire craft.
3. Motions of the craft are achieved by short bursts of 25 to 100 pound thrust rocket engines.

1

2.

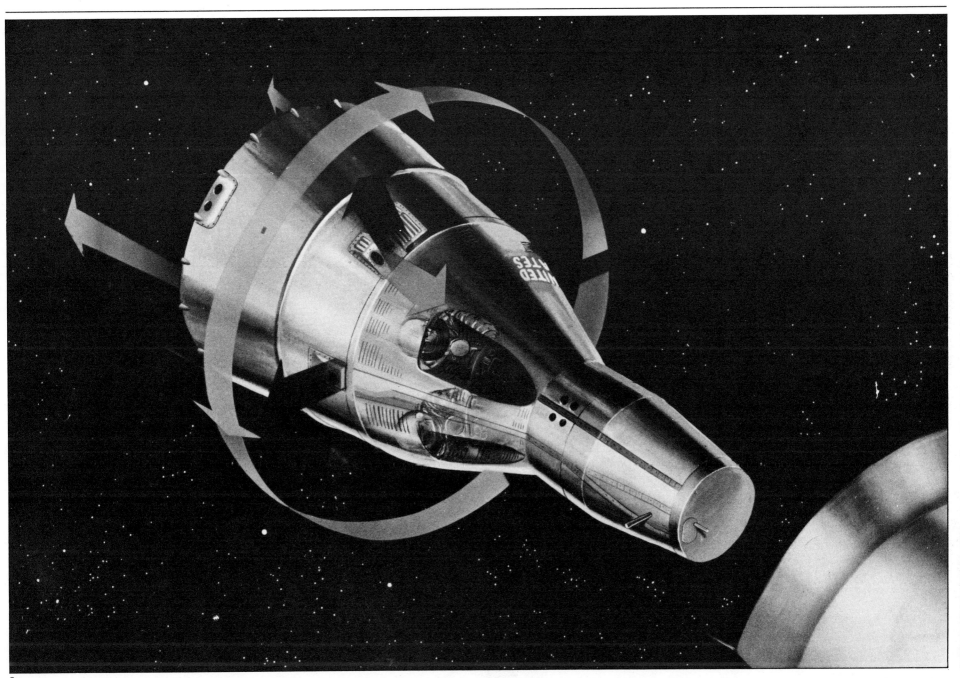

5. SPACE FASHIONS

Buck Rogers, his rakish "space helmet" securely in place, resolutely faces the rigors of space. Sometimes Buck wore a bubble helmet and oxygen supply, but he never bothered with a protective suit. Does Buck know something about surviving in the vacuum of space that we don't know? An Apollo helmet is worn by Frank Borman. It is a no-nonsense clear blister, under which Frank wears a soft cap, something like Buck's. The neat lock-fitting at the neck guarantees a pressure seal with the suit.

HOWDY, EARTHFOLKS!
BEST REGARDS
BUCK
ROGERS

Space Fashions

The fictional space travelers created by Cyrano, Verne and Wells ventured into space in their street clothes, unaware of the problems they would meet. By the 1930s, when Buck Rogers blasted off, men had been up in planes for a quarter of a century. The problem of maintaining a livable atmospheric pressure at high altitudes had become a working reality. In order to cope with the atmosphere problem, cabins, along with suits and helmets, had to be pressurized. If a cabin is not pressurized, then the suit must be.

Working in the vacuum of space, whether outside a spacecraft in flight or on the Moon, requires considerable costuming. The Apollo Moon suit, for example, consists of 21 layers of materials and has a system of ducts that provide air for breathing, pressure, and clearing of the face visor. It also distributes cool water by tubes to prevent the astronaut from overheating. Since the Moon's temperature can soar to over 500 degrees F, and there is no atmosphere to absorb the Sun's rays, the astronaut is extremely vulnerable. So that ground control can keep a constant check on his well-being, his suit is also wired to produce an electrocardiogram.

Some science fiction writers have done away with the cumbersome space suit altogether, substituting instead unobtrusive "force field" generators. These enable heroes and heroines to exist in the vacuum of space dressed in the height of 30th century fashion or—as in some recent tales—nothing at all.

For interior shipboard wear, the producers of the popular TV series *Space 1999* commissioned no less a figure than Rudi Gernreich to insure that their intrepid wanderers will face the unknown terrors of space in stylish comfort.

1. Buck Rogers was on the right track in the 1930s. Buck's tightly laced—and fashionable—boots anticipated the earliest attempts at space suits, and the influence of the G factor in liftoff and landing. He was also equipped with one of the first jet-packs, a weapon for fending off nasty aliens, and with grand, military-style pantaloons, stolen, it would seem, from the cavalry.
2. This version of the Gemini suit would make any self-respecting tailor cringe. The baggy knees and elbows are designed that way to allow the astronaut to move his arms and legs freely.

1

2

3. This is a prototype of what the well dressed man would wear for a walk in space. The life-support system is carried in the front. The jet-pack carried on the back is controlled by levers manipulated by hand.
4. This is an early NASA idea for a suit to meet prolonged exposure to the extreme temperatures and hard vacuum of the moon. Its many layers made it awkward. It looked more like a science fiction creation than many illustrations from science fiction itself. It never saw the light of the moon.

Fact Follows Fantasy
Buster Crabbe as Buck Rogers is at the controls in a (presumably) pressurized 1931 cabin. His no-nonsense clothing (note the neat headphone in the close-fitting cap) proved to be far ahead of its time. What Buck lacked in knee room and cushioning, he made up for in daring and good looks. An experimental suit produced in 1967 for Skylab by industrial designer Raymond Lowey and NASA, returns to all the comforts of home. Buck's cap and collarless tunic have become a reality.

3

4

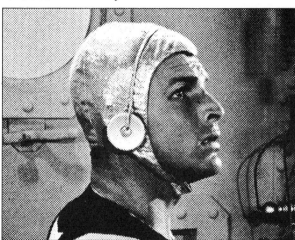

1. Why, you might ask, does that chap on the right have an over-turned garbage can on his head? And how did the fellows in the back get smeared with shaving cream? You meet some oddly dressed folk in space, especially in low-budget movies.
2. Raymond Massey emerges from his craft in the stunning 1936 film *Things to Come*. He looks vaguely as if he's wearing a radio vacuum tube on his head, but despite its bizarre appearance, it is very much in the tradition of today's helmets.
3. The two flight attendants in *2001* have arrived at a space "chic" far in advance of anything yet seen. Or are those portable hair dryers they're wearing? Still, the wasp-like padded hats appear appropriate to a weightless environment, especially in a later scene, when the ladies appear to walk upside down.
4. Buster Crabbe, as Flash Gordon, often sported unusual head-gear, including his own permanent wave. The romantic tradition of this 1930s space serial has been carried on in *Barbarella*, *Planet of the Apes*, and *Star Wars*.
5. A unique space helmet, inspired perhaps by Julius Caesar?

1

2

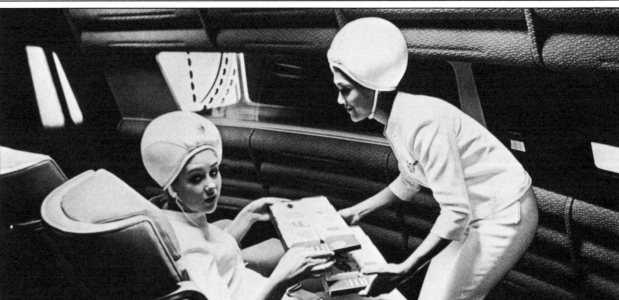

4

5

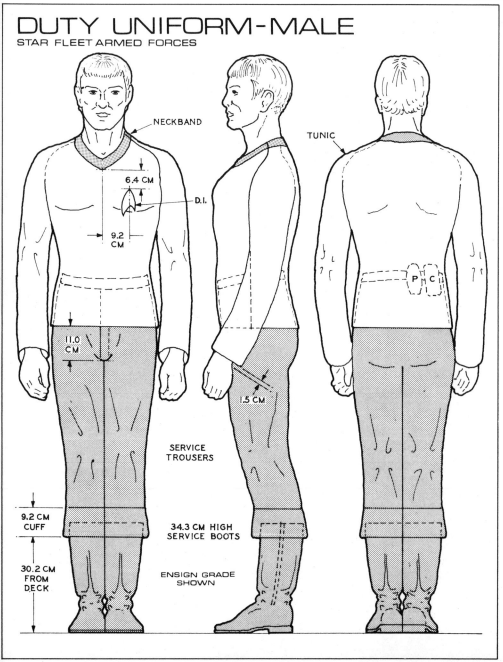

DUTY UNIFORM-MALE
STAR FLEET ARMED FORCES

NECKBAND

6.4 CM

D.I.

9.2 CM

TUNIC

11.0 CM

1.5 CM

P C

SERVICE TROUSERS

9.2 CM CUFF

34.3 CM HIGH SERVICE BOOTS

30.2 CM FROM DECK

ENSIGN GRADE SHOWN

1. The Star Trek duty uniform was designed thirty years after Buck Rogers and is contemporary with the development of NASA's Apollo flights. Buck's pistol has become a "phaser," his radio a "communicator." The duty uniform is worn, of course, in a fully pressurized Enterprise.
2. Edwin Aldrin on the Moon is here photographed in 1969 by Neil Armstrong. The rigors of space have forced the astronauts into a suit which appears encumbering, but proved to be quite successful in the reduced gravitational environment of the Moon. Aldrin's gold helmet visor reflects a part of the Lunar Module.
3. This schematic gives some idea of the complexity of the Moon suit. It is not so much a suit as an environment. The huge backpack is a small factory, working to maintain that environment.

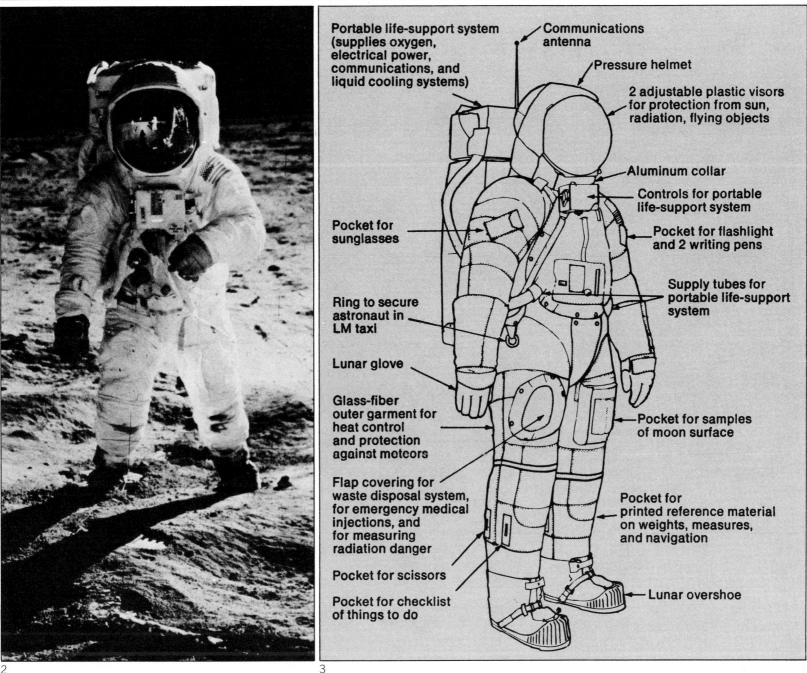

Portable life-support system (supplies oxygen, electrical power, communications, and liquid cooling systems)

Communications antenna

Pressure helmet

2 adjustable plastic visors for protection from sun, radiation, flying objects

Aluminum collar

Controls for portable life-support system

Pocket for sunglasses

Pocket for flashlight and 2 writing pens

Supply tubes for portable life-support system

Ring to secure astronaut in LM taxi

Lunar glove

Glass-fiber outer garment for heat control and protection against meteors

Pocket for samples of moon surface

Flap covering for waste disposal system, for emergency medical injections, and for measuring radiation danger

Pocket for printed reference material on weights, measures, and navigation

Pocket for scissors

Pocket for checklist of things to do

Lunar overshoe

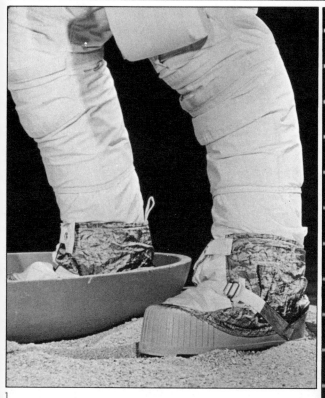

1. Apollo 11's Neil Armstrong shows off his strap-on Moon shoe, just the thing for a casual stroll on the lunar surface. It's disposable, so it keeps a fellow from tracking Moon dust back into the spacecraft.
2. Astronaut John Young (yes, that is a living man in there) wears the Gemini suit in a front and rear view. This suit had removable arms and legs, as well as a fold-aside fabric helmet for working in what NASA calls a "shirt-sleeve" environment. The various plumbing is for life-support and monitoring.
3. The Apollo hard inner-flight suit contains Eugene Cernan, commander of the Apollo 14 mission, here getting fitted for his flight. Minus the suit's white coverall, we get a good look at its advance design features.

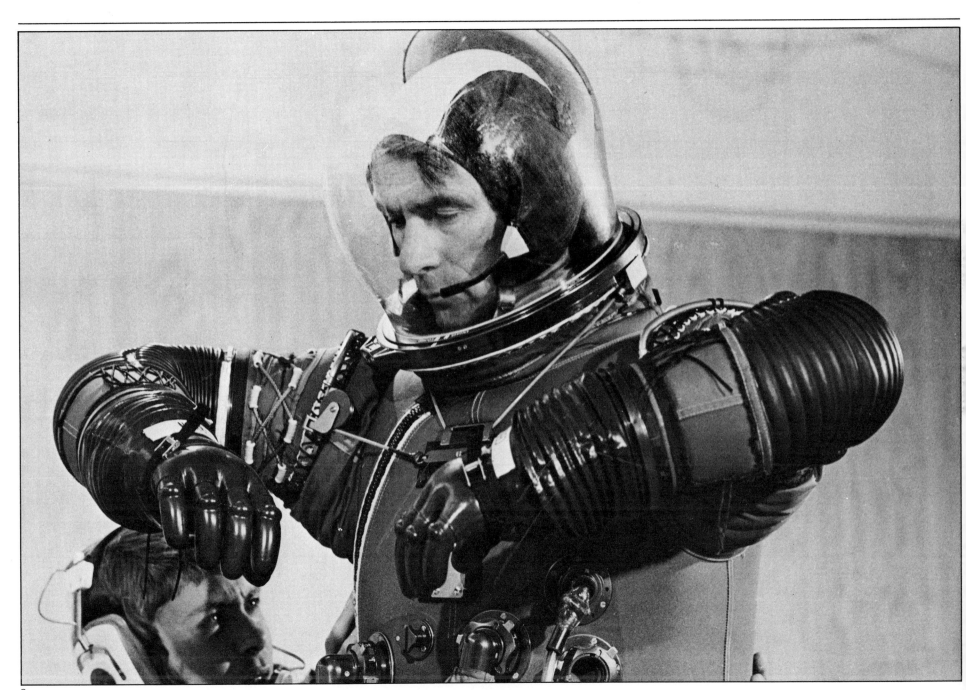

1. Accessories are handy for keeping an alien at bay. Or at least one eye is at bay. Both ray guns have the typical cooling fins. This drawing by Alex Schomberg features space travelers Gerry Carlyle and Anthony Quade in *The Seven Sleepers* by Barnes and Kuttner.
2. Should one venture into space without a ray gun? This sleek device has the added feature of being less cumbersome than the bracelet on the lady's arm. The romantic vision is by artist Stephen Lawrence for the 1948 *Fantastic Novel*. As for accessories, only the girls of science fiction seem to manage with wisps of nylon or less. But even these space travelers need watches, communicators and a spare ray gun or two. (You never know when an alien may be lurking in the zero-gravity toilet.)

1

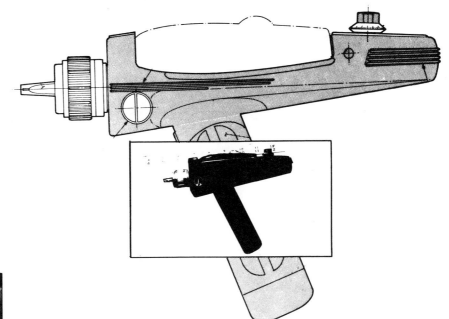

Fact Follows Fantasy

The Star Trek phaser is the space traveler's substitute for a Colt automatic. It is the only one of thousands of ray guns "invented" in science fiction. Laser technology is pretty much accepted as the norm in recent science fiction novels. In the 1974 novel, *The Mote In God's Eye* by Niven and Pournelle, a group of over-crowded aliens set up a bank of gigantic lasers. The immense blast of light-energy provides the thrust for a "light sail" thousands of miles in diameter. This sends their spaceship on its way, for all the world like a futuristic clipper ship or windjammer. The real laser, capable of melting its way through steel, or even diamonds, in seconds is now being researched for weapons technology. The rays from a laser consist of amplified electro-magnetic waves. Laser technology is derived from research in atomic structure.

1. For the well-dressed Moon walker, the Apollo 15 fills the bill. But just in case you forget anything, your left hand will have a checklist. And if you forget your left hand, your left leg has another checklist.

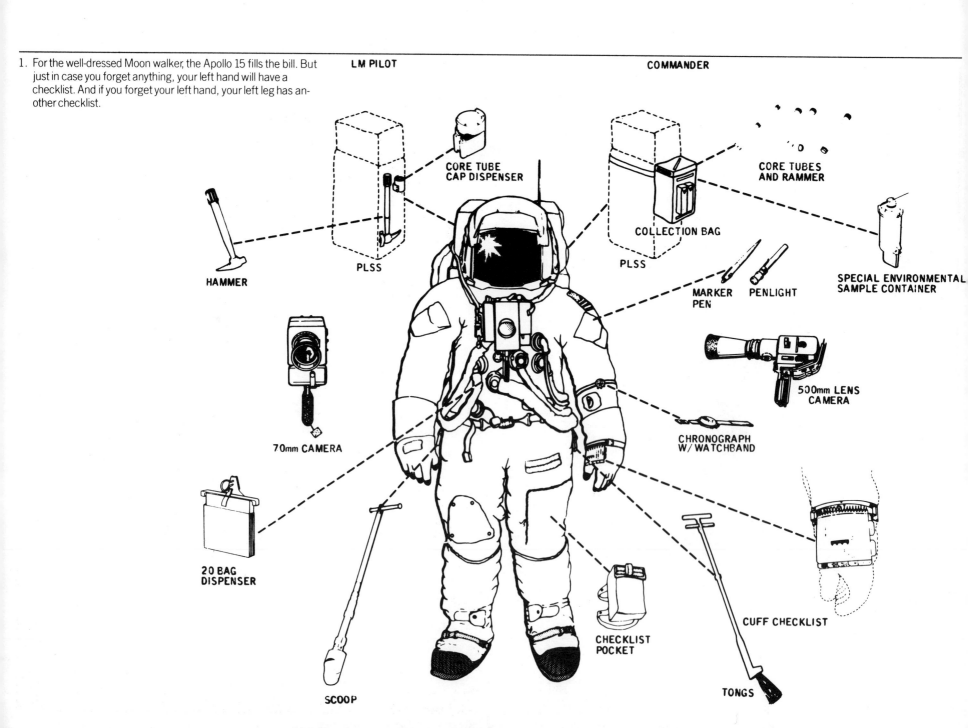

LM PILOT

COMMANDER

CORE TUBE CAP DISPENSER

CORE TUBES AND RAMMER

COLLECTION BAG

SPECIAL ENVIRONMENTAL SAMPLE CONTAINER

PLSS

PLSS

HAMMER

MARKER PEN

PENLIGHT

500mm LENS CAMERA

70mm CAMERA

CHRONOGRAPH W/ WATCHBAND

20 BAG DISPENSER

CHECKLIST POCKET

CUFF CHECKLIST

SCOOP

TONGS

Fact Follows Fantasy

A picture-taking robot-astronaut is prepared for a landing on the Moon in this first issue of *Rocket Stories* which appeared in 1953. He was followed in 1969 by a real-life astronaut Neil Armstrong, who like any smart tourist is checking out his camera before the trip.

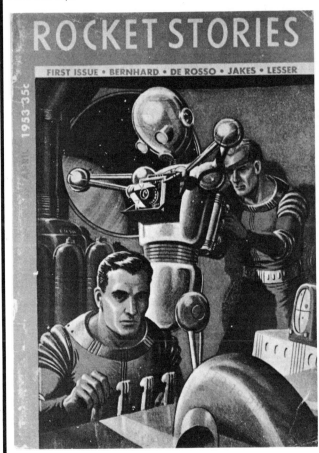

6. LIFE ABOARD

A scene from the 1936 British film *Things to Come* looked forward to a space age which provided generous interiors and costumes with a definitely romantic flair.

Life Aboard

Life aboard takes place within a pressurized cabin. The cabin's primary function is to protect the traveler from the vacuum of space. It also provides a regulated atmosphere, usually 60% oxygen and 40% nitrogen, a regulated heat and pressure, and protection from micro meteorites. Important too, it protects the occupants from radiation.

Life passes in a time frame no longer related to cycles of Earth time. There is no day or night as we know it. As you see the Earth rise up above the distant rim of the Moon, you know you are literally in another world.

Daily life takes place in a weightless condition that affects primary orientation and the carrying out of the simplest tasks. It can have short term comic effects. Watching a cookie crumble, for example, can mean one huge mess. During prolonged exposure to weightlessness, the muscles that go unused in lifting need regular exercise. Without it, they will begin to atrophy.

The number and variety of activities for the space traveler depend on the size and sophistication of the spacecraft. Space walks require special air locks and life support systems. Docking with other craft necessitates special controls and equipment. As in submarines, many areas have to serve multiple functions. For instance, early Mercury and Gemini flights required that the astronaut's driving seat be used for dining, washing up, and even as a toilet seat. Skylab, on the other hand, has separate sections of the craft for control, working, and personal functions.

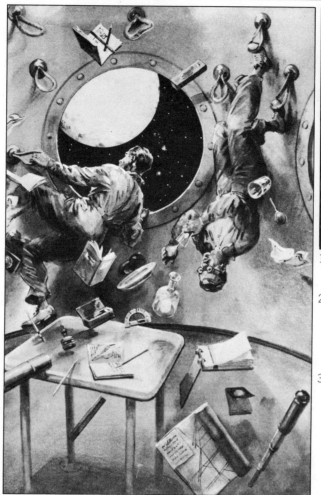

1

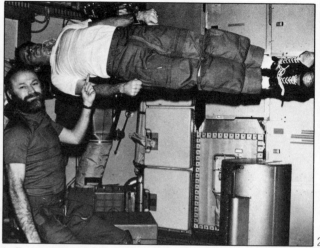

2

1. Two crew members from the science fiction story *In a Moon Bound Rocket* try to cope with zero gravity. They were obviously unprepared. Note the ever-present floating telescope.
2. A real-life view of weightless conditions on board Skylab 4. Astronaut Ed Gibson balances effortlessly on Gerry Carr's finger, performing a circus act impossible on earth. Can you imagine the feats that could be performed in a space Olympics? The astronauts lived for 84 days (a record) in this weightless environment without any lasting ill effects.
3. During a Skylab 3 mission, Astronaut Jack Lousma "flies" around in the orbital workshop's dome area. Hand-hold bars are widely distributed (as in many early science fiction renditions). Lousma and two other crewmen put in 59 days in the craft.

1

1. The passage of time and the advance of technology is vividly portrayed in these three interior images: Verne's Moon capsule, a Buck Rogers spacecraft, and the spaceship Discovery from the movie *2001: A Space Odyssey*. Victorian gaslight-plush evolves into a 1930s revolving chair with semi-circular art deco trim, then into a machine-like revolving core simulating gravity. The *2001* interior has an exercise ramp (note the jogging astronaut near the top of the picture), and a command station which houses the terminal of the infamous computer HAL. These images span 100 years and might give us some notion of what we might expect in the next 100 years. (Could we be seeing robots in an international frisbee match?)
2. Standing watch in the control room, the space travellers in the 1977 film *Star Wars* gaze out in astonishment at the awesome size of the Death star.

2

1. Astronaut "barber" Charles Conrad trims the hair of Skylab 2 Astronaut Paul Weitz in the orbital workshop wardroom, as Weitz wields the vacuum. The book behind them appears to be a Ray Bradbury science fiction classic. Without the vacuum, Weitz's hair would float about the cabin endlessly.
2. The body mass experiment rig gets a workout from astronaut Alan Bean aboard Skylab. This was one of many human engineering studies performed in space, to determine man's performance under weightless conditions over prolonged periods of time.
3. Skylab 3 astronaut Lousma demonstrating how to take a shower. The shower "curtain" is hauled up to the ceiling, completely enclosing him. A vacuum draws off even the smallest droplets of water.

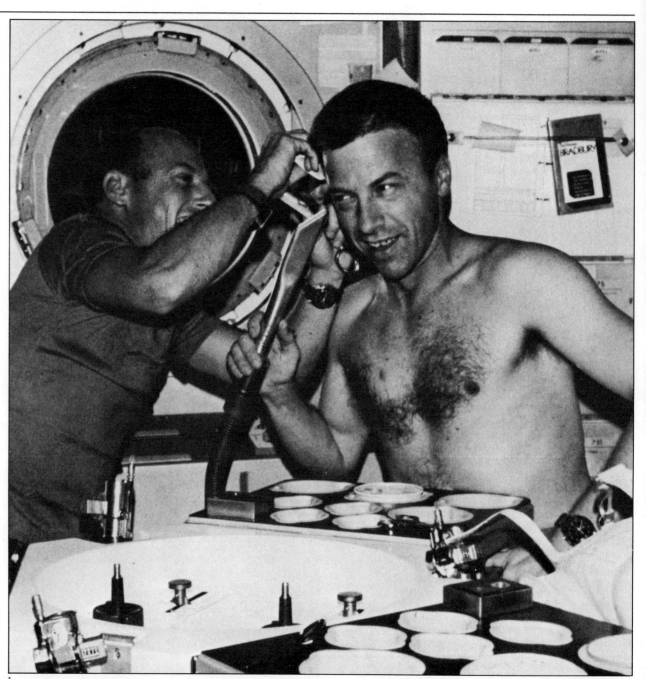

1

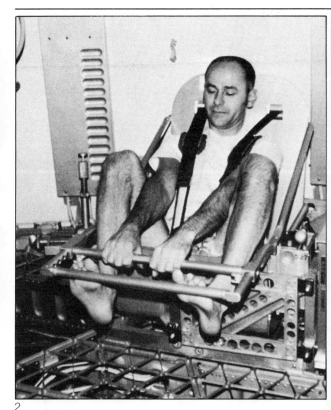

2

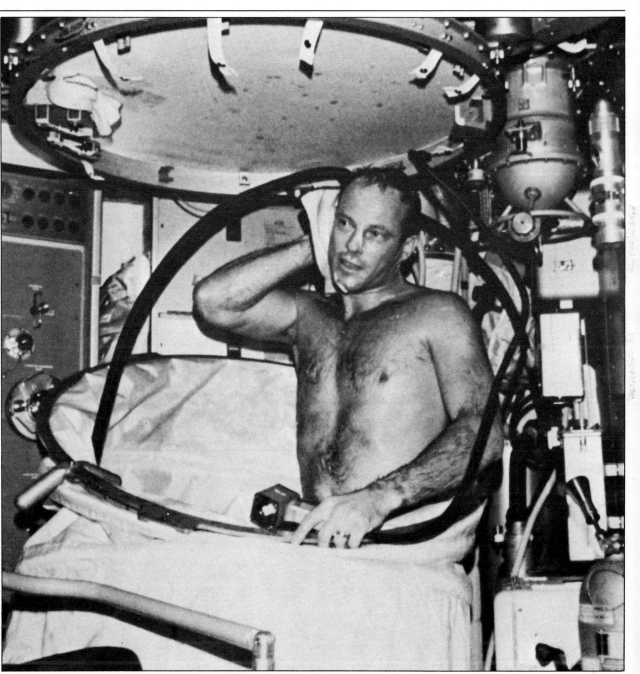

3

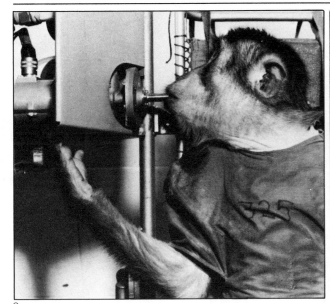
2

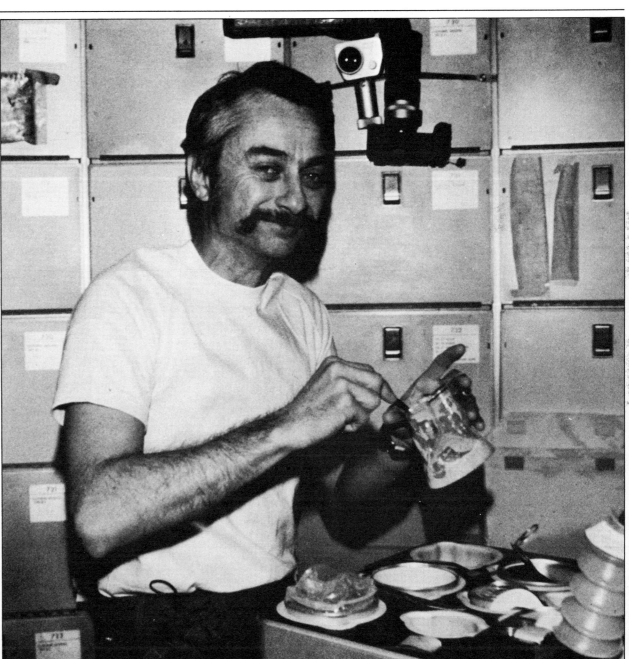
3

1. This is an early space program simulation of how to drink orange juice. It's a bit like sucking Crest out of its tube. Not suggested for a Thanksgiving turkey.
2. A pigtail monkey tests a water drinking device prior to a biosatellite flight. This monkey, No. 325, was preparing for a 30-day flight in space.
3. A relaxed astronaut, Owen Garriott of Skylab 3, reconstitutes food in the wardroom. (Presumably someone will eat the reconstituted food.) Note the pervasive presence of tape on the wardroom cabinets, a handy way to secure floating objects.

1. Mockup of early zero-gravity toilet.
2. The zero-gravity condition requires special handling for wastes. Part of that "handling" involves drying and storage in the large container on the left. NASA refers to the toilets as fecal collection units. They are, however, not mentioned in that biblical encyclopedia of space, *History of Rocketry and Space Travel* by Wernher von Braun and Frederick Ordway III. Too mundane a subject, perhaps.

2

1. Alan Bean reads in his bed, or "sleep restraint," in the crew quarters of Skylab 3. Behind his head is the ceiling.
2. A 1970 schematic of the interior of Skylab. The sleeping, eating and waste-disposal areas are all defined.
3. Astronauts could actually go to bed by zipping themselves upright in the sleep restraint. It is fastened at both ends to keep it from floating about.

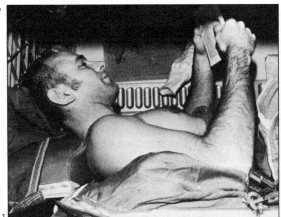

1

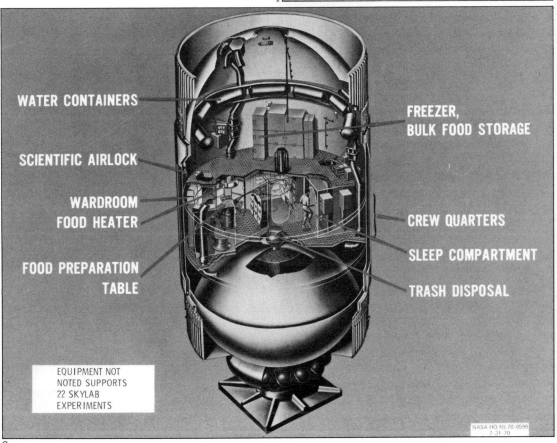

WATER CONTAINERS

SCIENTIFIC AIRLOCK

WARDROOM
FOOD HEATER

FOOD PREPARATION
TABLE

FREEZER,
BULK FOOD STORAGE

CREW QUARTERS

SLEEP COMPARTMENT

TRASH DISPOSAL

EQUIPMENT NOT
NOTED SUPPORTS
22 SKYLAB
EXPERIMENTS

NASA HO ML70-6599
7-31-70

2

3

7. TRIPS AND EXCURSIONS

A walk on the Moon, science fiction style, from *Frau im Mond*, the 1929 German movie. This is a pretty fair rendition of the event, some 40 years before the fact. Fritz Lang, with the advice of Hermann Oberth, had to build his set with construction sand.

Trips and Excursions

Trips and excursions in space fall into one of four mission categories: orbital, lunar, planetary, and in time, extra-solar or galactic. To date, orbital and lunar flights have been achieved by men. Planetary flights are still at the level of robot mechanisms (Viking, for example).

Stellar flights, like Pioneer 10 and 11, will leave our solar system, moving out "forever" in galactic orbit, silent witnesses to man's thus far miniscule achievements in reaching beyond the solar system. It should be remembered that the nearest star, other than our own sun, is light years away, and that light travels approximately six trillion miles in one year.

Space travel has already offered us spectacular views of our own Earth for the first time. It has given us images of the Moon and samples of its surface. It has offered us endless detailed photographs (reconstructed from television scanners) of the inner planets: Mars, Venus and Mercury, and, more recently, of the outer planet Jupiter. Soon we will have useful photographs of Saturn, but Uranus and Neptune will have to wait.

More has been learned in the past ten years about the heavenly bodies than in all past recorded time. Beyond the wealth of technical data, we have been able to observe marvelous phenomena. We have found on Mars alone a mountain higher than any on Earth, the longest and deepest canyon, and volcanoes beyond the imagination.

In addition to the Sun and its nine planets, we can now explore, or at least observe closely, the 33 available moons of these planets. These include the potato-shaped Martian moons, and the huge planet-sized moons of Jupiter. We can also rendezvous with any one of hundreds of asteroids, some of which, like Ceres, are larger than planetary moons. These asteroids may come in for considerable attention in the future because of their immense resources of precious materials.

Any manned trip beyond the solar system will involve more than just an extension of our existing technology.

1

It will require new propulsion systems, new human factors engineering, and new communication techniques. The distances that must be traveled are almost beyond the imagination. In the case of distant stars, a choice will have to be made between a form of suspended animation for the space travelers, or sustained generations of living persons aboard.

Building on the past, do we dare the future?

2

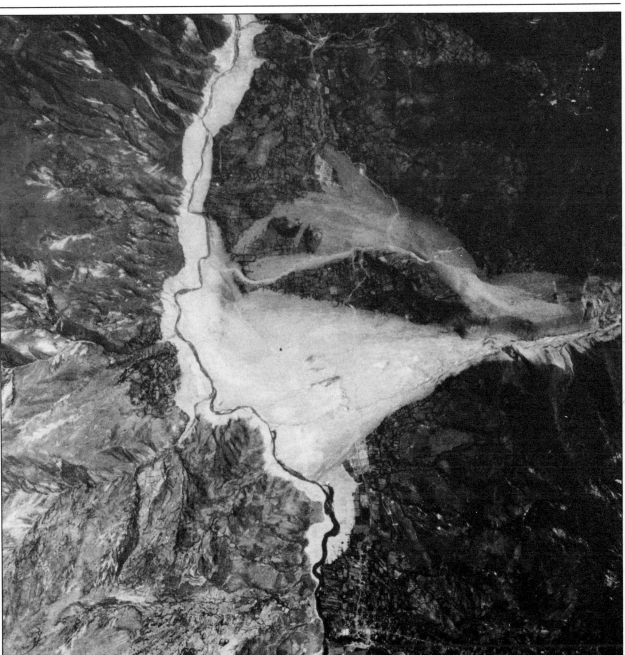

1. An Apollo photo shows Earthrise behind the Moon. Yes, that actually is the Earth, 230,000 miles away on the horizon.
2. A portrait of the Earth as photographed from Apollo 17. The coast of Africa and the Arabian Peninsula are outlined below scattered clouds.
3. An earthquake site in northern Peru was photographed by NASA to aid a Peruvian government study of a 1970 quake. High altitude photography has proved helpful in monitoring pollution and crop disease, locating mineral deposits and gaining an overview of the ebb and flow of life on land and sea.

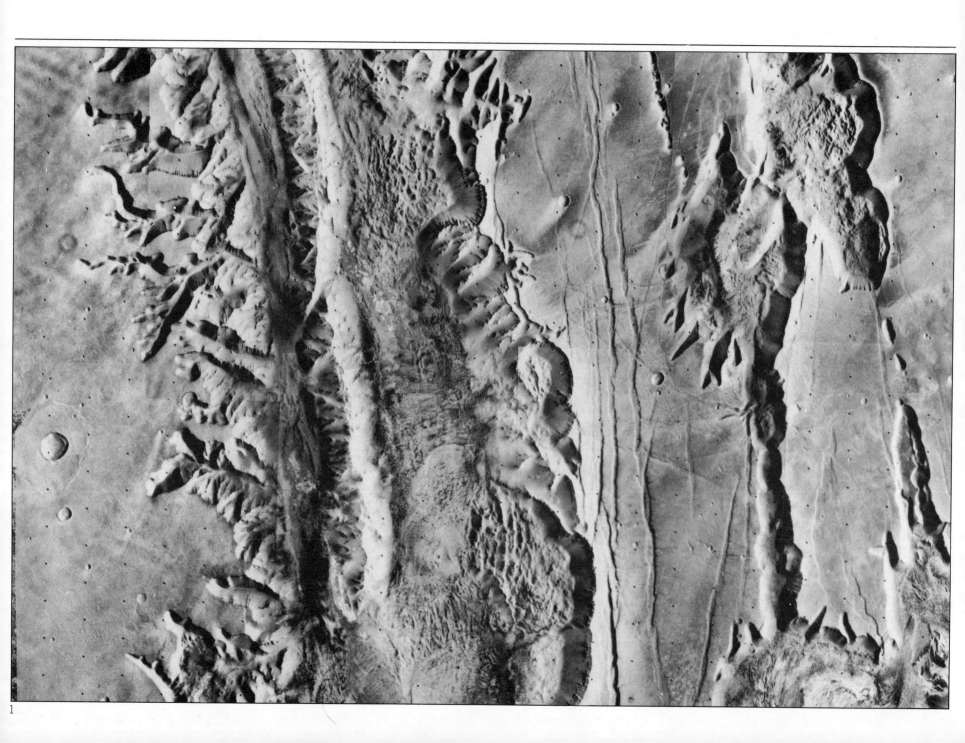

1. A composite picture of Mars and the gigantic canyon that stretches nearly one-third around the planet. The picture was taken at a distance of 2600 miles from the Red Planet.
2. A full Moon, in all its 2160-mile diameter, as caught by Apollo 11 during its homeward journey. The view is from 10,000 miles out.
3. This is Mariner 10's computer-enhanced television picture of an Earth-like Venus. The image was caught when the camera was 450,000 miles from the planet. Heavy clouds swirl around Venus' South Pole (bottom). As pleasant as it may look, Venus has a surface temperature of about 800 degrees F.
4. Jupiter has thirteen moons, of which four are shown in this artist's rendering. Cool Jupiter (minus 216 degrees F.) has been closely observed by the Pioneer 10 and 11 space probes. It is roughly 18 times the size of Earth, with an 88,700 mile diameter. Further study of Jupiter may take place via a program referred to as JOP: Jupiter Orbiter with Probe. Jupiter's four inner moons were discovered by Galileo in 1610.
5. Pioneer 11 is now on a 400 million mile flight to inspect and give us our first close look at the formidable Saturn and its rings. The artist's illustration depicts Saturn as it would appear from its largest satellite Titan.

2
3

4

5

Which is the Real Moon Vehicle?
Here are five candidates?

1. Prototype of the Mobility Test Article which was designed for prolonged exploration of the Moon. Each wheel had its own motor. The special wheels could handle both hard and soft Moon terrain.
2. A Mobile Laboratory vehicle developed for a study by the Bendix Corporation. This study cost $800,000, but the vehicle didn't make it.
3. A science fiction vehicle called *Moon Fargo* cruises through a field of styrofoam rocks.
4. Yes, it's the real Lunar Roving Vehicle.
5. The Mobile Geological Laboratory developed by General Motors was built to test procedures for exploring geological sites on the Moon. Here it investigates a California volcano crater.

Fact Follows Fantasy

Hugo Gernsback's *Amazing Stories* has the distinction of being the first science fiction magazine. Its inaugural issue appeared on April 5, 1926. An early cover of the magazine anticipates men walking on the Moon (*The Man Who Annexed the Moon*) with their spaceship in orbit and the Earth over their shoulders. When Edwin Aldrin stepped down on the Moon in 1969, he joined Neil Armstrong for a two hour and twenty minute walk. Neither man annexed the Moon, but they did plant an American flag and leave a message from the President.

1. The LRV (Lunar Roving Vehicle) is powered by electric batteries and carries two astronauts in light tubular seats. It has a ground-controlled television camera, a lunar communicator, high and low-gain antennae, tool pallet, lunar tools, and scientific measuring gear.
2. Packing up for a lunar trip requires more "baggage" than Richard Burton and Liz Taylor used to take along a trip. The Apollo 17 flight included the lunar module and the roving vehicle. The lunar module alone weighed in at 16 tons. It stood 22 feet 11 inches tall, and with its legs extended had a 31-foot diameter. It required one million parts in construction, including 41 miles of wire, six rocket engines, two radios, two radar sets and a sophisticated on-board computer.
3. Artist's conception of a 1990s mission to Mars. Included in the landing are two manned capsules, several Martian rovers, and three solar sail interplanetary shuttles. The lack of any clear evidence of life on Mars may put a damper on such an ambitious mission.

1

2

1. A mockup of the Viking Lander which touched down on Mars in 1976. Its most important observation and communication equipment are the S-band high gain antenna dish at the upper right; the meteorology sensor, protruding upwards in the center; cylindrically shaped cameras; the biological processor; and the surface-sampler boom and collector hand. Viking weighed in at 1320 pounds.
2. This is a close-up of Viking's "hand" digging into the Martian surface. Samples of the soil were then transferred to an automated organic chemistry lab aboard the craft.
3. An Apollo 15 lunar rock sample is here being processed in a nitrogen examination line. This rock has been classified as a blocky subangular varialitic gabbro, no less. It weighs 908.6 grams, about two pounds.
4. Astronaut Harrison Schmitt of Apollo 17 meets, not Moon Men on his EVA, but a huge split Moon boulder at the Taurus-Littrow landing site.

8. A SPACE ADVENTURE

What happens when fifty men and fifty women are sent on a one hundred year voyage through space to colonize another planet? Problems come up that even NASA might not anticipate. This ingenious strip-cartoon called *50 Girls 50* appeared in 1953 in William M. Gaines's *Weird Science* magazine.

I HAVE TO *LAUGH!* EVEN THOUGH MY FINGERS ARE GROWING NUMB AND I LIE PARALYZED IN MY DEEP-FREEZE SUSPENDED ANIMATION CHAMBER, FEELING THE INCREASING COLDNESS CREEPING OVER MY BODY AND KNOWING THAT *I AM GOING TO DIE,* I HAVE TO LAUGH. I WAS *FOOLED. I KNOW* THAT NOW. AND YET, WHEN MY BODY GROWS RIGID IN THE SUB-ZERO TEMPERATURE AND MY FLESH BECOMES BRITTLE AND THE LIFE LEAVES MY BODY, THERE WILL BE A *SMILE* FROZEN ON MY FACE. ONE YEAR AGO, I LAY LIKE THIS IN THIS VERY CHAMBER. ONLY THINGS WERE *DIFFERENT* THEN. THE COLD WAS *RECEDING* THEN. THE GROWING DARKNESS WAS VANISHING AND A WARMTH AND LIGHT WAS COMING OVER ME. FOR I WAS *THAWING.* I WAS *COMING TO.* I REMEMBER HOW I OPENED MY EYES AND SAT UP, PUSHING THE TRANSPARENT LID OPEN AND LOOKING AROUND AT THE TIERS OF OTHER D-F S.A. CHAMBERS WITH THEIR PALE-BLUE-FLESHED CONTENTS...

WE...WE'RE *TWO YEARS OUT OF EARTH.* PERFECT. *PERFECT.* JUST THE WAY I *PLANNED* IT.

I CLIMBED FROM MY CHAMBER, LISTENING TO THE SILENCE OF THE SHIP. I MOVED DOWN THE AISLE BETWEEN THE STACKED D-F UNITS AND PEERED INTO EACH, SMILING AT THE SCULPTURED STATUE-LIKE FACES OF THE WOMEN, AND SNEERING AT THE CLEAN-SHAVEN WHITE FACES OF THE MEN...UNTIL I CAME TO WENDY'S...

WENDY. BEAUTIFUL, DESIRABLE WENDY. THANK YOU, DARLING! THANK YOU FOR GIVING ME THE *IDEA* FOR ALL OF THIS. I'LL BE BACK TO *THAW* YOU IN A LITTLE WHILE...

THIS WAS WHAT I WANTED. THIS WAS THE BEGINNING OF MY PLAN. WENDY HADN'T ACTUALLY SUGGESTED IT. BUT SHE'D GIVEN ME THE IDEA. I PUT THE FIRST PHASE OF MY SCHEME INTO OPERATION AND RETURNED TO HER CHAMBER. I REACHED FOR THE TEMPERATURE CONTROL RELAY...THE SWITCH THAT WOULD SEND LIFE AND WARMTH INTO HER RIGID BODY. BUT THEN I HESITATED...

NO, DARLING! NOT *YET!* NOT YOU...*FIRST!* SOMEONE *ELSE.* AN *APPETIZER* TO THE *MAIN COURSE.* A *TEMPTER*...

I STEPPED TO THE NEXT TIER OF D-F UNITS AND SURVEYED THE FACES... THE FROZEN MASKS OF BEAUTY WITHIN. I FELT WILD AND ELATED AND MY BLOOD POUNDED THROUGH MY BODY. *FIFTY WOMEN!* AND I COULD *HAVE MY PICK*...

LAURA MASTERS. SHE'S... LOVELY. *LOVELY!* ALL RIGHT, LAURA. YOU WILL BE MY *FIRST CONQUEST*... MY *FIRST*...

I SHOVED THE RELAY FORWARD TO 'THAW'. THE REFRIGERATION UNIT KICKED OFF AND ANOTHER MOTOR CLICKED ON. I HURRIED BACK TO THE CONTROL ROOM AND SAT DOWN. IT WOULD TAKE A WHILE FOR LAURA TO COME TO...

FIFTY WOMEN. LET'S SEE. I'M *TWENTY-SIX* NOW. SAY I LIVE TO BE *SEVENTY*-SIX. THAT WOULD BE *ONE WOMAN EACH YEAR. HARDLY* ENOUGH TIME TO *TIRE* OF HER. HEH, HEH. WHAT A *LIFE* I'LL LEAD. WHAT *HEAVEN*...

WHILE I WAITED FOR LAURA'S THAWING TO BE COMPLETED, I THOUGHT OF HOW ALL THIS HAD COME ABOUT. MY VOLUNTEERING FOR THIS TRIP. I REMEMBER HOW WE ASSEMBLED, I AND THE FORTY-NINE OTHER MEN AND THE FIFTY WOMEN, AND LISTENED TO OUR FIRST BRIEFING...

LADIES AND GENTLEMEN. YOU HAVE BEEN CAREFULLY SCREENED AND PICKED FROM OVER *TWENTY-THOUSAND VOLUNTEERS* FOR THE *FIRST JOURNEY TO A DISTANT STAR*...

I REMEMBER HOW WE GASPED WHEN THE GENERAL TOLD US...

THE SOLAR SYSTEM WE HAVE CHOSEN, THE ONE THAT SEEMS MOST LIKELY TO CONTAIN AN INHABITABLE PLANET, WILL TAKE EXACTLY *ONE HUNDRED YEARS* TO REACH.

BUT... BUT WE WON'T *LIVE* THAT LONG...

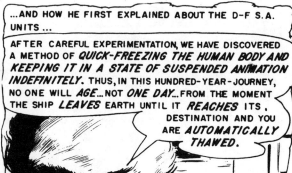

...AND HOW HE FIRST EXPLAINED ABOUT THE D-F S.A. UNITS...

AFTER CAREFUL EXPERIMENTATION, WE HAVE DISCOVERED A METHOD OF *QUICK-FREEZING THE HUMAN BODY AND KEEPING IT IN A STATE OF SUSPENDED ANIMATION INDEFINITELY.* THUS, IN THIS HUNDRED-YEAR-JOURNEY, NO ONE WILL *AGE*...NOT *ONE DAY*...FROM THE MOMENT THE SHIP *LEAVES* EARTH UNTIL IT *REACHES* ITS DESTINATION AND YOU ARE *AUTOMATICALLY THAWED.*

A SOUND BEHIND ME STARTLED ME FROM MY REVERIE. LAURA STAGGERED INTO THE CONTROL ROOM. SHE STARED AT THE CALENDAR-CLOCK. I ACTED SHOCKED AT SEEING HER...

OH, LORD! AT LAST! SOMEONE TO *TALK* TO! I THOUGHT I'D GO OUT OF MY *MIND* FROM *LONELINESS.*

WHAT *HAPPENED*? WE'RE *ONLY TWO YEARS OUT!* WE WERE SUPPOSED TO BE FROZEN FOR A *HUNDRED YEARS!*

I DREW HER TO ME, FEELING HER WOMANLY WARMTH, AND AMAZED AT MY ACTING ABILITY...

I'VE BEEN THAWED FOR *SIX MONTHS,* GOING *CRAZY* ALL BY MYSELF. MY *RELAY* FAILED. THAT'S WHAT HAPPENED TO *YOURS TOO.*

WE'LL... WE'LL HAVE TO *LIVE OUT OUR LIVES* ON THE SHIP...*DIE* OUT HERE IN SPACE...

THE GENERAL HAD MADE IT VERY CLEAR AT THE BRIEFING...

THIS *QUICK-FREEZE PROCESS* CAN *ONLY* BE DONE *ONCE.* THE *HUMAN BODY* CAN STAND *ONLY ONE FREEZE* AND *ONE THAW.* IF, FOR SOME UNFORSEEN REASON, ONE OF THE D-F UNITS *FAILED,* AND ONE OF YOU *CAME TO,* THERE WOULD BE *NO GOING BACK!* YOU WOULD LIVE YOUR LIFE OUT ON THE SHIP.

LAURA TREMBLED IN MY ARMS. MY FINGERS TINGLED, LONGING TO CARESS HER. BUT THAT WOULD COME. THIS WAS WHAT I WANTED. THE CHASE. THE CAPTURE. AND THEN, THE DELIGHTFUL ENJOYMENT OF SURRENDER...

OH, *SID.* WHAT WILL WE *DO?*

AT LEAST THERE'S THE *TWO* OF US, LAURA. WE CAN SEE IT THROUGH *TOGETHER!*

HOW MANY TIMES DOES A MAN DREAM OF BEING MAROONED ON A DESERT ISLAND WITH A BEAUTIFUL WOMAN? NOW, FOR ME, THE DREAM HAD COME TRUE. MAROONED ON A ROCKET-SHIP-ISLAND...IN SPACE...WITH LAURA...

SID... I'M *FRIGHTENED.* HOLD ME TIGHTER. *KISS ME!*

BABY...

INSTEAD OF THE ROAR OF BREAKERS ON A SILVERY BEACH, THERE WAS THE HUM OF NINETY-EIGHT D-F UNITS. INSTEAD OF SWAYING PALMS, THERE WERE NINETY-EIGHT FROZEN BODIES, TIERED ONE OVER THE OTHER DOWN THE AISLE. BUT WE WERE *ALONE* ON OUR ROCKET-SHIP-ISLAND. *ALONE AND UNINHIBITED...*

OH...DARLING!

SWEET...

BUT SOON, THE SILVERY BEACH TURNED GREY AND FLOTSAM-STREWN. THE BEAUTIFUL WOMAN TURNED UGLY. THE TINGLING LEFT ME. I WAS *TIRED* OF LAURA. IT WAS *TIME*...

SID. WHAT *IS* IT? WHAT'S THE *PARALYZER* FOR?

I'M *THROUGH* WITH YOU, LAURA. IT'S BEEN ALMOST A *YEAR* AND I'M *SICK AND TIRED* OF YOU. I WANT *SOMEONE ELSE*...

I REMEMBER HOW SHE LOOKED AT ME, AND THE REALIZATION CAME TO HER...

YOU... *YOU* THAWED ME! YOU DID IT ON *PURPOSE*. YOU WANTED *COMPANY*. YOU WANTED ...*OH, GOD*... AND NOW YOU'RE *BORED*...

THAT'S *RIGHT*, LAURA. AND AFTER YOU'RE *BACK* IN YOUR FREEZE-CHAMBER... *DEAD*...I'LL THAW ONE OF THE *OTHERS!*

SHE CURSED ME AS THE PARALYZER BLAST MADE HER BODY GROW RIGID. I CARRIED HER BACK TO HER D-F UNIT AND SET THE RELAY BACK. SHE WOULD NEVER WAKE UP. THE REFREEZING WOULD KILL HER...

THANKS, LAURA! THANKS FOR THE *APPETIZER*.

I DUMPED HER IN AND SHUT THE LID... 3

I WAITED UNTIL THE COLOR DRAINED FROM HER FACE AND THE BLUENESS STIFFENED HER AND SHE LOOKED LIKE A FINELY CHISELED PIECE OF SCULPTURE. ONE COULD NOT TELL THAT SHE WAS NO LONGER IN THE SUSPENDED-ANIMATION STATE, BUT ACTUALLY DEAD. THAT IS, IF ONE DIDN'T LOOK TOO CLOSELY AT WHERE THE TEARS HAD TURNED TO ICE ON HER CHEEKS...

PERFECT! NOW...FOR *YOU*, WENDY! THE...*MAIN COURSE!*

I STARED IN AT DESIRABLE WENDY...PALE AND DEATH-LIKE, WITH SENSUOUS BLUISH LIPS, WENDY...WHOSE HOT BLOOD HAD BEEN STOPPED COLD AND NOW LAY AS RIGID RED ICE-WIRES ENCASED IN SUB-ZERO HARDENED VEIN AND ARTERY AND CAPILLARY WALLS. WENDY... WHO I WANTED SO MUCH THREE YEARS AGO. WENDY, WHO NOTICED MY HUNGRY LOOKS AND CAME TO ME ONE DAY...

YOU'RE NAME IS *SID*, ISN'T IT? I'VE BEEN *WATCHING* YOU FOR *SOME TIME*...

I'VE BEEN WATCHING *YOU TOO*, WENDY! YOU'RE... *VERY BEAUTIFUL!*

I REMEMBER THE GENERAL'S WORDS. I REMEMBER HOW HE'D PREDICTED WENDY'S AND MY MEETING...

YOU ARE FIFTY MEN AND FIFTY WOMEN. YOU HAVE BEEN *CHOSEN CAREFULLY.* YOUR *MENTALITY...* YOUR *PHYSICAL ATTRIBUTES... ALL* OF YOUR *QUALITIES* HAVE BEEN CONSIDERED. BUT WHAT IS *MORE IMPORTANT...*EACH OF YOU HAS A *PERFECT MATE* IN ONE OF THE *OPPOSITE SEX GROUP...*

THE GENERAL WENT ON TO EXPLAIN... ABOUT PSYCHOLOGICAL FACTORS... TEMPERAMENT RATIOS...INTELLIGENCE LEVELS. I LOOKED AROUND, LAUGHING TO MYSELF. *ANY ONE* OF THEM...

ONCE YOU *REACH* YOUR DESTINATION AND BEGIN BUILDING YOUR *COLONY,* YOU WILL *FIND* YOUR MATE. IT IS *INEVITABLE.*

I PUSHED THE RELAY OF WENDY'S D-F UNIT TO 'THAW'...

WENDY...MY *MATE!*

THE GENERAL HAD BEEN RIGHT! IN FACT, WENDY AND I HAD GOTTEN TOGETHER *BEFORE* THE TAKE OFF...SHE WAS *CRAZY* ABOUT ME...

YOU'RE IN CHARGE OF THE D-F UNITS, AREN'T YOU, SID? *INSTALLING* THEM... *SETTING THE RELAYS?* NO ONE CAN *TAMPER* WITH THEM?

NO ONE... EXCEPT *ME! WHY?*

IT WAS TRUE. EACH OF US HAD BEEN ASSIGNED TO SOME PART OF PREPARING THE SHIP FOR THE TRIP. MY ASSIGNMENT HAD BEEN THE DEEP-FREEZE SUSPENDED ANIMATION CHAMBERS...

COULD YOU *SET* A RELAY TO *THAW* SOMEONE *BEFORE* THE HUNDRED YEARS ARE UP, SID, DARLING?

I'D HAVE TO *REWIRE IT...* MAKE SOME *ADJUSTMENTS...* BUT IT *COULD* BE DONE! *WHY?*

DARLING. DO YOU REMEMBER WHAT THE *GENERAL* SAID... ABOUT *FINDING YOUR MATE...?*

YOU *MEAN..?*

I LOVE YOU, SID...

BABY...

NO! *WAIT!* THERE'S *PLENTY* OF TIME FOR *THAT!* LISTEN TO MY *PLAN!*

YOUR... *PLAN?!*

THE COLOR WAS COMING INTO WENDY'S CHEEKS NOW. SHE WAS THAWING. SUDDENLY I THOUGHT OF IT. SHE'D BE FURIOUS, KNOWING THAT I HADN'T WAITED TILL TWO MONTHS BEFORE ARRIVAL-DATE...

BUT *WHY*? WHY *MAKE* HER ANGRY? SHE WANTS TO BE *QUEEN OF THE COLONY!* WHY LET HER *KNOW* WE'RE ONLY *THREE YEARS OUT*?

I WENT BACK TO THE CONTROL-ROOM AND CHANGED THE CALENDAR-CLOCK TO *98 YEARS OUT*...

I'LL TELL HER I MADE A *MISCALCULATION*. THAT WE *ARRIVE* IN *TWO YEARS*. BY *THEN* I OUGHT TO BE *TIRED* OF HER, AND WANT TO *MOVE ON*!

I SAT DOWN TO WAIT. IT WOULDN'T BE LONG BEFORE WENDY WAS IN MY ARMS. I GRINNED...

SHE THINKS I AGREED TO *HER* PLAN. SHE...

WENDY WAS STANDING AT THE DOORWAY TO THE CONTROL ROOM. SHE HAD A PARALYZER IN HER HAND...

WENDY...BABY! I...I WHAT'S *THAT*?

IT'S A *PARALYZER*, BUSTER! IT'S FOR *YOU*...

6

BUT, *BABY!* OUR PLAN! *YOUR* PLAN... TO BE KING AND QUEEN OF THE COLONY.

HAH! I'LL BE *QUEEN* ALL RIGHT, BIG BOY! BUT NOT WITH *YOU* AS KING!

WENDY!

I *NEVER LOVED YOU*, YOU *FOOL*. I *USED* YOU... GOT YOU TO *THAW ME* BEFORE THE *OTHERS*. YOU'RE GOING *BACK INTO YOUR CHAMBER!*

I'M GOING TO *RE-FREEZE* YOU! YOU KNOW WHAT *THAT* MEANS...

IT'LL *KILL* ME!

SHE RAISED THE PARALYZER. I FELT THE BLAST STIFFEN ME...

WEN...

SO LONG, SUCKER!

EXACTLY! AND DO YOU KNOW WHAT I'M GOING TO DO AFTER YOU'RE *DEAD*? I'M GOING TO *THAW OUT THE GUY I REALLY LOVE*. THE GUY I *PLANNED* ALL THIS WITH!

WENDY... HAVE PITY!

I HAVE TO *LAUGH!* EVEN THOUGH I'M *DYING*, I HAVE TO LAUGH. I WAS *FOOLED*, ALL RIGHT. BUT I HAVE TO LAUGH BECAUSE *WENDY'S* GOING TO FIND OUT THAT *SHE'S BEEN FOOLED TOO*. SHE'S GOING TO FIND OUT THAT SHE'S ONLY *THREE YEARS OUT*... THAT SHE'LL *NEVER LIVE* TO BE *QUEEN* OF THE COLONY! AND THE *PAY-OFF*... WHEN SHE *THAWS* HER *'REAL LOVER'*... SHE'S GOING TO WATCH HIM TURN *PUTRESCENT!* YOU SEE, THE *FIRST* PHASE OF MY SCHEME WAS TO *KILL EVERY MAN ON THE SHIP*...

AND NOW I'M GETTING SLEEPY. IT'S GROWING DARK AND I CAN'T FEEL ANYTHING. JUST *ONE* THING BOTHERS ME. *LAURA!* WHY DID I PICK *HER FIRST... OVER WENDY?* HMMMMM...

THE END 7

9.THE FUTURE

The Sun's corona reveals the wispy structure of its outer reaches. The sun, properly viewed (eye protection is essential), is a spectacular sight. Studies of the Sun's structure will be critical in energy development on Earth in the decades ahead. The Sun is our closest star at 90 million miles from the Earth. Its surface area is 11,920 times larger than that of Earth, and its mass is 332,488 times larger. An awesome object.

The Future

Although Earth communications and energy needs will dominate the field of rocketry in the near future, the emphasis in the long run will probably change over to space travel, space stations and space settlements.

After a decade or more of important investigation and discovery by both manned and unmanned spacecraft, there has been a growing interest in actually living and working in space on a permanent basis. Some of the questions being asked are the feasibility and goals of colonization, its scale and physical configurations, and its means of support.

There is also the question as to who will direct this mission. Will it be the scientific/educational sector, the business/industrial or the organizational/governmental group?

The era of pilot personalities and engineers is over. The non-astronaut space traveler will soon have his turn. The future of space then will fall to mankind at large.

No one knows for certain what our adventures in space will hold. Will we alter our physical or psychological states? The astronauts in Skylab discovered that over prolonged stays in space, they stretched an inch or more in height when the pressure was removed from the disks of their spines. And is there a possibility that we could ever make contact with other intelligent beings? Whatever else we may think, we can at least know we have finally crossed over the ultimate frontier.

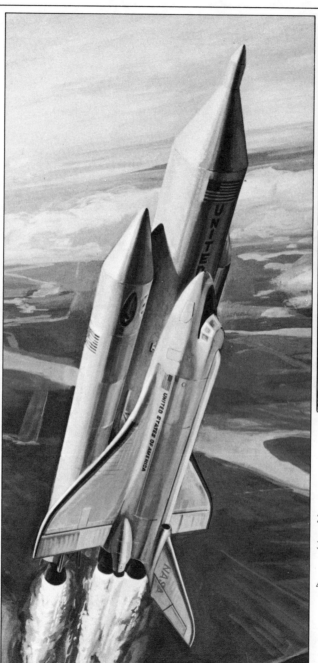

1

2

3

Space Shuttle

1. For the next five years, the $9.5 billion Space Shuttle program will be the dominant concept in the US space effort. It will ferry men, tools and machines to orbital missions. It will be lofted by twin solid propellant booster rockets that deliver a combined thrust of 5,300,000 pounds, plus its own three on-board 470,000 pound thrust engines.
2. The central ET (external tank) will carry fuel for the launch. It is jettisoned after the solid boosters, which are recoverable.
3. The Space Shuttle ejects its payload. The payload might be an orbiting lab, orbiting telescope, or energy station. Assembly of components or modules can then take place.
4. After its orbital mission, the Shuttle will gradually reduce its 17,000 mph orbital speed on re-entering the atmosphere. It will land at a mere 180 knots on a runway here on Earth. The Shuttles will therefore be reusable. Each launch will cost something like $20 million. By NASA calculations, this is less than half the cost of conventional spacecraft launches. The first manned Shuttle flight is expected to take place in 1979.

1. Artist's rendering of possible future configurations. In this three-engine model, nuclear energy would supply the thrust needed for deep space missions.
2. A delta-shaped craft would carry a manned mission to Mars. The nose module would lift off from Mars and return the astronauts to Earth.
3. This three-part vehicle-craft for Martian exploration combines outboard nuclear rockets and a central section containing the command module, landing module and return module.

AIR BREATHING

NUCLEAR

RECOVERABLE
UPPER STAGE

NASA R 67-1349
12-22-66

Fact Follows Fantasy

This daring fellow with his sail, chute and ballast basket dates from 1871. He flies out of a book called *Southern Discovery by a Flying Man* by Restif de la Bretonne. Is that a pressure suit he's wearing? The solar sailor Yankee Clipper has been designed as a means to study Halley's comet on its next Earth approach in 1986. The 700 meter square sail of aluminized plastic would collect energy (photon radiation) to power the space station. Such a station could be lifted into orbit in sections by the Space Shuttle, then assembled in space.

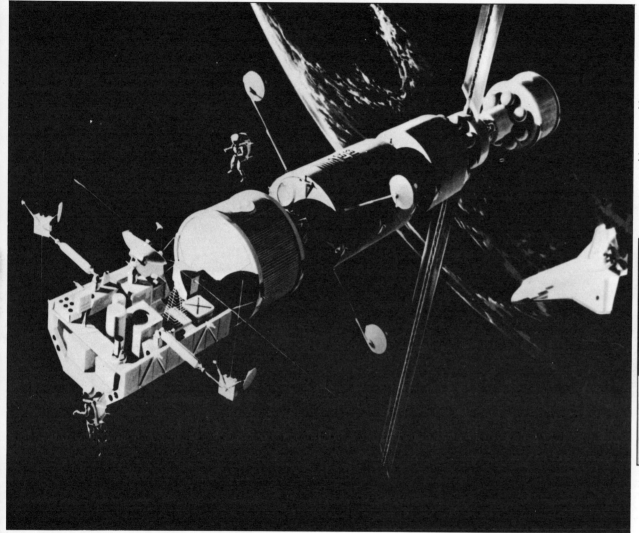

Stations

1. This proposed space station, serviced by the Space Shuttle, is built around the technology developed for Skylab and other space programs. It would be used to study life sciences and experiment with space manufacturing on a commercial basis. It could also store cargoes of instruments and materials, and act as a base for the construction of larger orbital structures.

2. An X-Y-Z axis orbital space station is surrounded by a cluster of support and observation modules. It would permanently rotate around its axis to simulate a minimum gravitational field for the station crew.

3. An early (and somewhat romantic) concept by NASA of an orbiting space station. It would rotate about an axis to simulate a gravity environment. It contains all the comforts of home, if your home is a bit Spartan. The craft is reminiscent of Tsiolkovsky's early spacecraft (see p. 16) and Oberth's designs for *Frau im Mond* (p. 23).

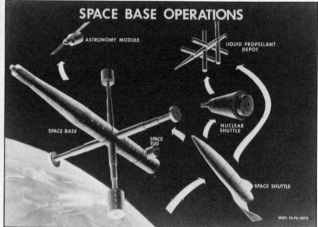

1

2

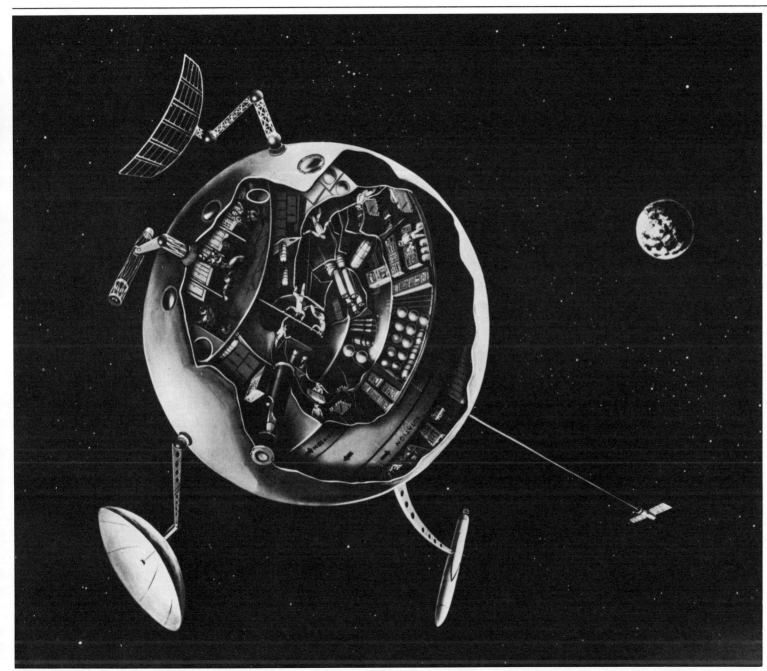

1. The imaginations of 19th century Englishmen soared when this engraving for a rocket balloon was published. Its gondola took the shape of a boat, possibly for an unhappy landing at sea.
2. The idea of an inflated craft carried into the 1960s, with this model of a rotating torus for a space station. The toroid shape has distinct advantages because this shape can easily be stabilized in rotation to create artificial gravity. The shape is a recurring theme in science fiction and science fact. In the film *2001*, Kubrick made magnificent use of it in his giant wheel-like space station. It is still a favorite in today's space colony studies.

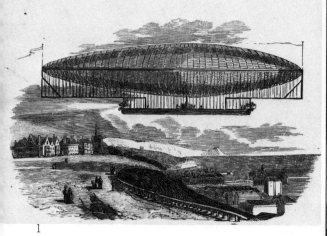

1

2

1. The ultimate space colony? This gigantic interior landscape within a space station is based on the work and speculation of Dr. Gerard O'Neill of Princeton. About 100,000 inhabitants would live and work in a 19 mile long cylinder with a diameter of four miles. This project might cost in the neighborhood of $150 billion. (Nice neighborhood!) The colony would not have a bridge (at least one the size of the San Francisco Golden Gate). This has been added to the picture only to give you an idea of the enormous scale of the project.

2. A view down the 19 mile long cylindrical interior of O'Neill's space colony shows the meandering landscape, framed above by gigantic windows looking out into space. Huge mirrors would furnish solar power, regulate the seasons, and control the day-night cycle. Rotation every 114 seconds along the cylinder's axis would simulate gravitation for the inhabitants and their environment. A "pioneer" group of inhabitants would help build the structure from materials mined from the Moon and possibly an Asteroid belt.

1

2

1. This is a rendering of a vast torus space colony which was designed at Stanford University. The colony would support upwards of 10,000 inhabitants. The structure is a mile in diameter. The interior quarters for living and working would have a diameter of two hundred yards, with an interior view from one side to the other of half a mile. The interior (as in Dr. Gerard O'Neill's concepts) would have a very Earth-like appearence, with sunlight, flowers and trees. The reigning theory is, of course, that an Earth-like ambiance would be less disturbing to the colonists. What looks like rocks on the side of the torus *are* rocks—a thick coating of Moon rocks which act as an immense shield against cosmic radiation. The overhead flat torus (upper right) acts as a reflector for sunlight. The sunlight is angled down into the central ring of mirrors for conversion to electrical energy. It would provide the power the colony needs, with enough left over to carry out useful work. The colony would orbit the Earth at about the same distance as the Moon, and draw on the Moon for many of its basic materials.

'2. An angular section, through the outer torus ring, exposes at the top chevron-shield mirrors that reflect the sun's rays into the colony, while baffles shield out the cosmic rays. The top interior level contains modular housing (by its appearance, almost directly borrowed from Expo '67's Habitat). The housing will be interspersed with open-space parks. A track visible at left will provide transportation. A second level will house the service area, including storage, power distribution, and some equipment for light industry.

3

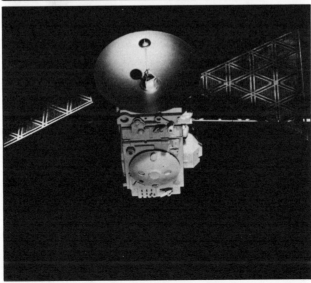

4

3. Central core docking and communication center of the Stanford Space Colony. The sphere at the center is 130 meters in diameter and might be called the Grand Central Station of the colony. It acts as a terminal for the radiating transportation spokes and the space port tower. The cantilevered extensions on the tower are docking stations, while the dish at the top is an antenna for Earth communication.

4. Factory complex associated with the Stanford Space Colony concept. Mined Moon materials would be processed into glass, metals and other strategic materials. A connecting tube would provide transportation access to the main colony. The triangular wings on either side of the complex convert solar rays into electrical energy for the factory.

1. Hugo Gernsback wrote his novel *Ralph 124C41 +* in 1911 for *Modern Electrics* magazine. That was nearly a cool fifty years before actual manned flight. In that novel, Gernsback, with unusual clairvoyance predicted (as described by James Gunn in *Alternate Worlds*) "space travel, plastics, florescent lighting, jukeboxes, liquid fertilizers, loud speakers, flying saucers, sleep learning, solar energy, radar, rustproof steel, microfilm, television, radio networks, skywriting, hydroponics, tape recorders, aquacades, vending machines, night baseball, cloth made of glass, and synthetic fabrics." All that back in 1911! His hero Ralph is seen here entering a space capsule and being received by a dubious fellow traveler.

2. The movie *2001* is the realization of Gernsback's dream in further fictional imagination. By 1968, with the team of Kubrick and Clarke, a great deal more authority is attached to the visualization. The full range of on-going technological hardware was pushed to the extreme heights of imagination. Depicted here is the moment following separation of the pod-lander from the spaceship Discovery and its descent toward the planet Jupiter.

3. A 1976 Ames Research Center scheme for a space habitat carries out the long chain of imagination and accomplishment from Cyrano to Gernsback to Clarke. New spokesmen Gerard O'Neill, Carl Sagan, and Richard Johnson are carrying their ideas into highly technical and soon feasible ventures. The central sphere of this colony is a mile in circumference and houses the inhabitants. At either end of the complex are docking facilities and manufacturing modules.

1

2

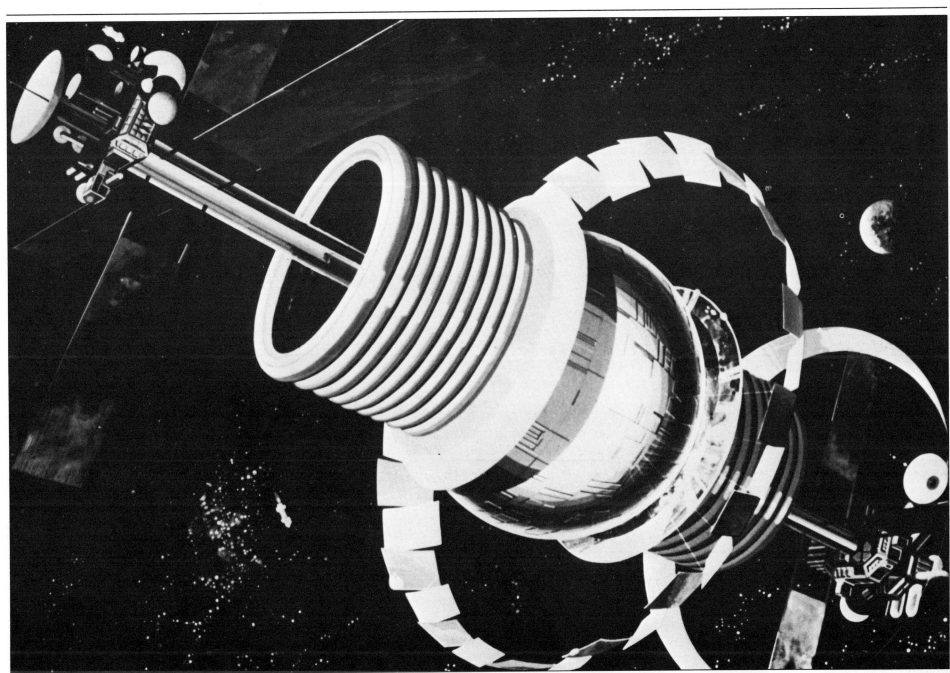

Terminology

Apogee: Highest point reached in orbit.

Atmosphere: The blanket of gases surrounding a planet.

Booster: The rocket which delivers the propulsion for a lift-off.

Burn: Firing of a rocket engine during flight.

Docking: Link-up after rendezvous, of two spacecraft.

Escape velocity: Speed required to overcome gravitational pull.

Extravehicular Activity (EVA): Work outside a spacecraft.

Gyroscope: An instrument which maintains directional orientation.

Missile: Any object designed to travel in a trajectory to a target.

Perigee: Lowest point reached in orbit.

Pitch: Up and down motion of a craft.

Propellant: Mixture of fuel and oxidizer which produces thrust.

Retrorocket: Rocket fired opposite to the direction of a craft's motion.

Staging: Planned firing and separation of rocket motors in flight.

Thrust: Force generated by burning gases in rocket engine.

Trajectory: Course through atmosphere or space.

Tumbling: End-over-end motion of a craft

Yaw: Side-to-side motion of a craft

Zero-gravity: Point at which weightlessness occurs.

Bibliography

Agel, Jerome (editor), *The Making of Kubrick's 2001,* N.Y. The New American Library, 1970.

Braun, Wernher, von and Ordway, F.I., *History of Rocketry and Space Travel,* N.Y., Crowell, 1975 (revised).

Braun, Wernher, von and Ordway, F.I., *The Rockets' Red Glare,* N.Y., Anchor Press/Doubleday, 1976.

Braun, Wernher, von, *Space Frontier,* N.Y., Holt, Rinehart and Winston, 1971 (revised).

Clarke, Arthur, C., *Man and Space,* N.Y., Time Inc., 1965.

Clarke, Arthur, C., *The Promise of Space,* N.Y., Harper & Row, 1968.

Clarke, Arthur, C., *Profiles of the Future,* N.Y., Harper & Row, 1963.

Clarke, Arthur, C., *2001 a Space Odyssey,* N.Y., The New American Library, 1968.

Emme, Eugene, M., *A History of Space Flight,* N.Y., Holt, Rinehart and Winston, 1965.

Frewin, Antony, *One Hundred Years of Science Fiction Illustration,* N.Y., Pyramid Books, 1975.

Gunn, James, *Alternate Worlds* (An illustrated history of science fiction), N.J., Prentice Hall, 1975.

Kyle, David, *A Pictorial History of Science Fiction,* London, Hamlyn Publishing Group Limited, 1976.

Ley, Willy, *Rockets, Missiles and Men in Space,* N.Y., Viking, 1968.

Sadoul, Jacques, *The Year 2000* (illustrations from the golden age science fiction), Paris, editions Denoël, 1973.

Shelton, William, R., *Man's Conquest of Space,* Washington, D.C., National Geographic Society.

Smolders, Peter, *Soviets in Space,* N.Y., Taplinger Publishing Co. Inc., 1973 (revised).

Stoiko, Michael, *Soviet Rocketry,* N.Y., Holt, Rinehart and Winston, 1970.

Sullivan, Walter, *America's Race for the Moon,* N.Y., Random House, 1962.

Whitfield, Stephan, E., *The Making of Star Trek,* N.Y., Ballantine Books, 1968.

Wilford, John, Noble, *We Reach the Moon,* N.Y., Bantam Books, 1969.

Wipple, Fred, L., *Earth, Moon and Planets,* Cambridge, Mass., Harvard University Press, 1963.

Acknowledgements

We would like to thank the following sources for their permission to print illustrations in this book. In case of discrepancy, please contact the publishers. Corrections will be made in subsequent editions.

A Pictorial History of Science Fiction, by David Kyle, London, Hamlyn Publishing Group Ltd., 1976: p. 51 (2); 62 (1).

Alternate Worlds, by James Gunn, N.J., Prentice-Hall, 1975: p. 79 (1).

Buck Rogers: The Collected Works of Buck Rogers in the 25th Century, N.Y., Chelsea House Publishers, 1969: p. 20 (1); 33; 54 (2); 67 (1); 68 (1); 84 (1).

Encyclopedia of Source Illustrations, N.Y., Morgan & Morgan, Inc., 1972: p. 9.

Francois d'Allegret: p. 41 (1).

History of Rocketry and Space Travel, by Wernher von Braun and Frederick I. Ordway, III, N.Y., T.Y. Crowell, Inc., 1975 (revised): p. 26 (1,2); 27 (1).

Martin Marietta Corporation: p. 3; 27 (2); 37 (2); 40 (1); 52 (1); 77 (3).

Metro-Goldwyn-Mayer: p. 29 (2); 44 (1); 61 (2); 71 (3); 84 (1); 124 (2).

Museum of Modern Art: p. 15; 70; 71 (2,4,5); 81.

National Aeronautics and Space Administration, Washington, D.C.; p. 18 (1,2); 19 (1,2); 28 (2); 30 (2); 31 (2); 35 (2); 36 (1); 38 (1,2); 39 (3); 40 (2,3); 41 (2,3); 45; 49 (1,2); 50 (1,2); 52 (2); 55 (2); 60 (1); 61 (2); 62 (2); 63 (1); 64 (1,2); 65; 67 (2); 68 (2); 69 (3,4); 73 (2,3); 74 (1,2,3); 75; 78 (1); 79 (2); 82 (2); 83; 86; 87 (2,3); 88; 89 (2,3); 90 (1,2); 91 (1,2,3); 94; 95 (2,3); 96; 97 (2,3,4,5); 98 (2,4); 99 (2); 100 (1,2); 101; 102; 103 (2,3,4); 113; 114 (1,2,3); 115; 116 (1,2,3); 117 (2); 118 (1,2); 119; 120 (2); 121 (1,2); 122 (1,2); 123 (3,4); 125 (1).

National Air and Space Museum of the Smithsonian Institution, Washington, D.C.: p. 12 (1); 13 (1,2); 14 (1,2); 17 (1,2); 21 (2); 22 (2,3); 23 (1,2,3); 24 (1); 25 (2); 29 (1); 34 (1,2); 37 (3); 47 (1); 48 (1,2); 51 (3); 54 (1); 55 (1); 57; 59; 82 (1); 84 (1); 93; 98 (1,3,5); 99 (1); 120 (1); 124 (1).

New York Public Library: p. 1; 5; 10; 22 (1); 42 (1); 44 (2); 69 (5,6); 76 (1,2); 117 (1).

New York Times: p. 18 (3); 28 (3); 30 (1).

The Rocket's Red Glare: An Illustrated History of Rocketry Through the Ages, by Wernher von Braun and Frederick I. Ordway, III, N.Y., Doubleday & Co., Inc., 1976: p. 12 (2).

Soviets in Space, by Peter Smolders, N.Y., Taplinger Publishing Co., Inc., 1974: p. 16 (1,2,3); 28 (1); 35 (1); 51 (1).

Stamps, Posts and Postmarks, by Ian Angus, N.Y., St. Martin's Press, 1973: p. 31 (1).

The Star Trek Star Fleet Technical Manual, Ballantine Books: p. 72; 77 (1,2).

Twentieth Century Fox: p. 85 (2).

U.S. on the Moon, Washington, D.C., U.S. News and World Report, 1969: p. 58 (1).

U.S. Navy: p. 27 (3).

William M. Gaines's *Weird Science Magazine,* N.Y., William M. Gaines, 1977, for strip cartoon "50 Girls 50," pp. 105-111.